70119568

TALES FROM GRIMM

OTHER BOOKS BY WANDA GÁG AVAILABLE FROM

THE UNIVERSITY OF MINNESOTA PRESS

THE ABC BUNNY

THE FUNNY THING

GONE IS GONE

MORE TALES FROM GRIMM

NOTHING AT ALL

SNIPPY AND SNAPPY

SNOW WHITE AND THE SEVEN DWARFS

TALES FROM GRIMM

FREELY TRANSLATED
AND ILLUSTRATED BY
WANDA GÁG

University of Minnesota Press
Minneapolis • London

The Fesler–Lampert Minnesota Heritage Book Series

This series reprints significant books that enhance our understanding and appreciation of Minnesota and the Upper Midwest. It is supported by the generous assistance of the John K. and Elsie Lampert Fesler Fund and the interest and contribution of Elizabeth P. Fesler and the late David R. Fesler.

Copyright 1936 by Wanda Gág
Copyright renewed 1964 by Robert Janssen

Originally published in hardcover by Coward–McCann, Inc., in 1936

First University of Minnesota Press edition, 2006

All rights reserved. No part of this publication may be reproduced, stored in a retrieval system, or transmitted, in any form or by any means, electronic, mechanical, photocopying, recording, or otherwise, without the prior written permission of the publisher.

Published by the University of Minnesota Press
111 Third Avenue South, Suite 290
Minneapolis, MN 55401-2520
http://www.upress.umn.edu

Library of Congress Cataloging-in-Publication Data

Gág, Wanda, 1893-1946.
    Tales from Grimm / freely translated and illustrated by Wanda Gág.
    — 1st University of Minnesota Press ed.
        p. cm. — (The Fesler-Lampert Minnesota heritage book series)
    Summary: An illustrated collection of sixteen tales, including "Hansel and Gretel" and "Rapunzel."
    ISBN-13: 978-0-8166-4935-8 (hc/j : alk. paper)
    ISBN-10: 0-8166-4935-9 (hc/j : alk. paper)
    ISBN-13: 978-0-8166-4936-5 (pb : alk. paper)
    ISBN-10: 0-8166-4936-7 (pb : alk. paper)
    1. Fairy tales—Germany. [1. Fairy tales. 2. Folklore—Germany.]
    I. Grimm, Wilhelm, 1786–1859. II. Grimm, Jacob, 1785–1863. III. Title.
PZ8.G123Tal 2006
[398.2]—dc22

2006016241

Printed in the United States of America on acid-free paper

The University of Minnesota is an equal-opportunity educator and employer.

30 29 28 27 26 25 24   12 11 10 9 8 7 6 5

TO FOUR FRIENDS

INTRODUCTION

*T*HE *magic of* Märchen *is among my earliest recollections. The dictionary definitions—tale, fable, legend—are all inadequate when I think of my little German* Märchenbuch *and what it held for me. Often, usually at twilight, some grown-up would say, "Sit down, Wanda-chen, and I'll read you a* Märchen." *Then, as I settled down in my rocker, ready to abandon myself with the utmost credulity to whatever I might hear, everything was changed, exalted. A tingling, anything-may-happen feeling flowed over me, and I had the sensation of being about to bite into a big juicy pear.*

When, four years ago, I was in the midst of a Hansel *and* Gretel *drawing, the old* Märchen *magic gripped me again and I felt I could not rest until I had expressed in pictures all that* Märchen *meant to me.*

In order to be influenced as directly as possible by the real spirit of these stories, I read them in the original German. I had at that time no idea of writing my own text but I soon found that I wanted to do this also.

After choosing a group of stories, I made literal translations of them. Some lent themselves easily to this method and came out practically as fresh and lively as they were in the original. This was especially true of those in dialect, for, because of their simple language and many repetitions, they were clear enough for any child to understand. Others, which were smooth, warm and colorful in the original, came out thin, lifeless and clumsy. It seemed evident that in the case of the latter, only a free translation could convey the true flavor of the originals. I hoped it might be possible—and thought it worth trying—to carry over into the English some of their intimate me-to-you quality, and that comforting solidity which makes their magic more, rather than less, believable.

The fairy world in these stories, though properly weird and strange, has a convincing, three-dimensional character. There is magic, wonder, sorcery, but no vague airy-fairyness about it. The German witches are not wispy wraiths flying in the air— they usually live in neat cottages and wear starched bonnets and spotless aprons. The bear in Snow White *and* Rose Red *is only outwardly bewitched, for a rent in the fur reveals him as a fully dressed, flesh-and-blood Prince underneath. The story of the* Spindle, Shuttle *and* Needle *is more airy than most, but even here the supernatural agents are not ballet-skirted fairies with wands, but three plain workaday objects. Aside from this, many of the stories are folk tales rather than fairy stories—and what could be more substantial than a peasant?*

The oftener I read these stories, the more I longed to delve into their backgrounds. Upon doing so, I realized for the first time that a great number of the tales are not exclusively German, but exist in the folk lore of many other countries and civilizations. Also, in many cases, there is no one authentic version of a story. There are many recurring motifs which are used inter-changeably, resulting in an endless number of combinations, some of them perfectly formed, others overbalanced or incomplete.

The Brothers Grimm were as much interested in collecting disjointed fragments as they were complete stories. Sometimes they presented a story as they found it, carefully labeling it as hybrid or incomplete; but more often they used two or more imperfect stories, adding and subtracting various units to make a well rounded whole.

The title Kinder-und Hausmärchen *(Nursery and Household Tales) indicates that the material was not written exclusively for children. The fairy tale age-limit has shifted considerably since 1812, when these tales were first collected, and has probably dropped two years more since I was a child. At fourteen I was still avidly reading fairy tales and hopefully trying out incantations; but in this sophisticated age of the movies, radio, tabloids, and mystery stories, one cannot set the fairy tale age limit over eleven or twelve. I do not believe in "writing down" to children, but since the stories were originally written to include adults, it seemed advisable to simplify some sections in order that a four-to-twelve age group might be assured of getting the full value of the stories.*

By simplification I mean:

(a) freeing hybrid stories of confusing passages

(b) using repetition for clarity where a mature style does not include it

(c) employing actual dialogue to sustain or revive interest in places where the narrative is too condensed for children.

However, I do not mean writing in words of one or two syllables. True, the careless use of large words is confusing to children; but long, even unfamiliar, words are relished and easily absorbed by them, provided they have enough color and sound-value.

The tales, coming as they do from many sources, and being composed by such widely different people as peasants and scholars, are written in a great variety of styles and tempos, which I have tried to preserve in every case.

On the matter of "goriness" in juvenile literature there are, of course, conflicting opinions. As I did not want to rely solely on my own judgment, I consulted several authorities. The general opinion was that too much bowdlerizing creates a spineless quality which is not characteristic of these tales, and that more depends on the method of narration than on the actual details of such episodes. A certain amount of "goriness," if presented with a playful and not too realistic touch, is accepted calmly by the average child. In this way sanguinary passages can be rendered harmless, without depriving them of their salt and vigor.

Finally, I hope that the following annotations will show that, while I found it advisable to make free translations of some of the stories, I did not carelessly make free with the material at hand. In their scholia, the Brothers Grimm point the way to what is authentic and legitimate. Moreover, they have brought *such a thorough and ethical attitude to their task, that no one, after reading their painstaking annotations, could with a clear conscience shuffle their material indiscriminately.*

Hansel and Gretel *is probably the most characteristic and best beloved of all the stories. While there are variants of it, the one given preference by the Grimms is the most familiar. I have followed it almost to the point of making a literal translation, but have drawn upon the Bechstein version (specifically endorsed by the Grimms) for a few minor touches, such as that of the birds and the gems—and my story has a slightly different ending from either. Those who know the story through Humperdinck's opera may feel disappointed at not finding such characters as the gingerbread children and the sandman, but as they are not mentioned either in the main or alternative versions, I could not include them.*

Six Servants *is not as well known as it deserves to be, probably because of the inclusion of superfluous material and an anticlimax, making it hard to remember. Stripped of these, it is such a perfect tale that I feel justified in simplifying the story, using the essential units and leaving the unimportant ones in that relative obscurity where the whole story has remained up to this time.*

There are many versions of the Frog Prince. *One of these, sanctioned by the Brothers Grimm, has the ending which I have used. In it, too, the incident about Iron Henry is omitted.*

Clever Elsie *is one of the stories which lent itself easily to literal translation. The episode in the rye-field is one of several patterns which is tacked on to a certain type of story—always about a stupid girl. I used an alternative ending because I felt it would be easier for children to understand. The one usually used with this story involves the explanation of an old custom, without which Hans' behavior is unaccountably heartless.*

In The Three Brothers *I could not resist using the gnat episode which is quoted by the Grimms as a legitimate substitute for the horse-shoeing feat.*

The anecdote at the end of Lazy Heinz *seemed superfluous and was therefore omitted.*

Many people appear to be under the impression that there is only one Cinderella—*the godmother and pumpkin-coach version. But there is no one authentic story of Cinderella. It is one of the most widespread and mutable tales in the whole collection. Not only has it many variants in the German, but it exists in one form or another in the folklore of many countries, such as the English, French, Italian, Greek, Scandinavian, Serbian and Egyptian. I have adhered to the main Grimm version in all the important parts, using alternative patterns in only a few minor passages, chiefly for purposes of clarity. The familiar pumpkin-coach version is not included even in the alternative variants. Therefore it cannot be called a Grimm* Märchen *and I did not feel justified in using it.*

The Fisherman and His Wife *is in dialect and was apparently written down word for word as it was told. The diction and imagery are that of a peasant, its form is perfect. I made a very*

*direct translation, changing neither the style nor form. I was
familiar with this story before I could read and was enchanted
with the fisherman's supplication to the fish. I understood very
little of it literally—but in spite, or perhaps because, of this, it
was potentially fraught with magic meaning for me. Here it is
in dialect:*

> *Manntje, Manntje, Timpe Te,*
> *Buttje, Buttje in der See*
> *Myne Fru de Ilsebill*
> *Will nich so as ik wol will.*

*It was this lilting rhyme which made all things possible in the
story for me, and that is why I have preserved as many of its
magic sounds as possible in my translation. In some variants the
man and his wife start out living in a wooden hut and that is the
way it is usually translated. In the original they begin in a much
worse place—a chamber pot—but in still another version it is a
vinegar jug. In one story, as in mine, the supernatural agent is
a golden fish instead of a flounder.*

In the original of Doctor Know-It-All *the peasant's name is*
Krebs (Crab) *and was apparently chosen so that it could be
punned upon at a critical point in the story. But our idiomatic
equivalent of* Du Armer Krebs! *is* You poor fish! *Hence my substitute of that name for the other.*

Milford, New Jersey,
Summer, 1936.

xiii

ACKNOWLEDGMENT

For critical advice and friendly help in reaching original source material, I wish to thank Anne Carroll Moore and Mary Gould Davies of the New York Public Library, Anne T. Eaton, of The Lincoln School, Teachers College, Columbia University, and Carl Zigrosser of the Weyhe Galleries in New York. I am also grateful to Irita Van Doren and May Lamberton Becker of "Books" the New York Herald-Tribune, for whom I made the Hansel and Gretel drawing which finally led to the Tales from Grimm.

W. G.

TABLE OF CONTENTS

CONTENTS

LIST OF FULL PAGE ILLUSTRATIONS

HANSEL AND GRETEL

HANSEL AND GRETEL

IN a little hut near the edge of a deep, deep forest lived a poor woodchopper with his wife and his two children, Hansel and Gretel.

Times were hard. Work was scarce and the price of food was high. Many people were starving, and our poor woodchopper and his little brood fared as badly as all the rest.

One evening after they had gone to bed, the man said to his wife, "I don't know what will become of us.

All the potatoes are gone, every head of cabbage is eaten, and there is only enough rye meal left for a few loaves of bread."

"You are right," said his wife, who was not the children's real mother, "and there is nothing for us to do but take Hansel and Gretel into the woods and let them shift for themselves."

She was a hard-hearted woman and did not much care what became of the children. But the father loved them dearly and said, "Wife, what are you saying? I would never have the heart to do such a thing!"

"Oh well then," snapped the stepmother, "if you won't listen to reason, we'll all have to starve." And she nagged and scolded until the poor man, not knowing what else to say, consented to do it. "May heaven keep them from harm," he sighed.

Hunger had kept the children awake that night, and, lying in their trundle-beds on the other side of the room, they had heard every word their parents had said. Gretel began to cry softly but her brother Hansel whispered, "Don't worry, little sister; I'll take care of you."

He waited until the father and mother were sleeping soundly. Then he put on his little jacket, unbarred the back door and slipped out. The moon was shining brightly, and the white pebbles which lay in front of the house glistened like silver coins. Hansel bent down and gathered as many of the shiny pebbles as his pockets would hold. Then he tiptoed back to bed and told Gretel he had thought of a very good plan for the morrow.

At break of day the mother came to wake the children. "Get up, you lazy things," she said, "we're off to the forest to gather wood. Here is a piece of bread for each of you. Don't eat it until noon; it's all you'll get today."

Gretel carried both pieces of bread in her apron because, of course, Hansel's pockets were so full of pebbles. They were soon on their way to the forest: the mother first with a jug of water, the father next with an ax over his shoulder, Gretel with the bread and Hansel bringing up the rear, his pockets bulging with pebbles. But Hansel walked very slowly. Often he would stand still and look back at the house.

"Come, come, Hansel!" said the father. "Why do you lag behind?"

"I'm looking at my little white kitten, papa. She's sitting on the roof and wants to say good-by."

"Fool!" said the mother. "That's not your kitten. That's only the morning sun shining on the chimney."

But Hansel lingered on and dropped the pebbles behind him, one at a time, all along the way.

It was a long walk, and Hansel and Gretel became very tired. At last the mother called a halt and said, "Sit down, children, and rest yourselves while we go off to gather some wood. If you feel sleepy you can take a little nap."

Hansel and Gretel sat down and munched their bread. They thought their father and mother were nearby, because they seemed to hear the sound of an ax. But what they heard was not an ax at all, only a dry branch which was bumping against a dead tree in the wind.

By and by the two little children became so drowsy they lay down on the moss and dropped off to sleep. When they awoke it was night and they were all alone.

6

"Oh Hansel, it's so dark! Now we'll never find our way home," said Gretel, and began to cry.

But Hansel said, "Don't cry, little sister. Just wait until the moon is out; I'll find the way home."

The moon did come out, full and round and bright, and it shone on the white pebbles which Hansel had strewn along the way. With the glistening pebbles to guide them, they found their way back easily enough.

Dawn was stealing over the mountains when they

reached their home, and with happy faces they burst in at the door. When their mother saw them standing before her, she was taken aback. But then she said, "Why, you naughty children! Where have you been so long? I began to think you didn't want to come back home."

She wasn't much pleased but the father welcomed them joyfully. He had lain awake all night worrying over them.

·　　·　　·　　·　　·

Luckily, things now took a turn for the better, and for several weeks the woodchopper was able to earn enough money to keep his family from starving. But it did not last, and one evening the children, still awake in their trundle-beds, heard the mother say to the father: "I suppose you know there's only one loaf of bread left in the house, and after that's eaten, there's an end to the song. We must try once more to get rid of the children, and this time we'll take them still deeper into the woods, so our sly Hansel can't find his way back."

As before, the father tried to talk her out of it, but the hard-hearted stepmother wouldn't listen to him. He who says A must also say B, and because the father had given in the first time, he had to give in this time as well.

Hansel saw that he would have to get up and gather pebbles again, and as soon as his parents were asleep, he crept out of bed. But alas! the door was locked now and he had to go back to bed and think of a different plan.

The next day everything happened as it had the first time. Hansel and Gretel were each given a crust of bread and then they all went forth into the forest. Hansel brought up the rear as before, and kept straggling behind the rest.

"Come, come, Hansel!" said the father. "Why do you lag behind?"

"I see my pet dove, papa. It is sitting on the roof and wants to say good-by to me."

"Fool!" said the mother. "That's not your dove. That's only the morning sun shining on the chimney."

But Hansel kept on loitering because he was again

9

busy making a trail to guide them back home. And what do you think he did this time? He had broken his bread-crust into tiny pieces and now he was carefully scattering the crumbs, one by one, behind him on the path.

They had to walk even farther than before, and again the parents went to gather wood, leaving Hansel and Gretel behind. At noon Gretel shared her bread with Hansel, and then they both fell asleep.

When they awoke, it was dark and they were all alone. This time Gretel did not cry because she knew Hansel had scattered crumbs to show them the way back. When the moon rose, Hansel took her hand and said, "Come, little sister, now it's time to go home."

But alas! when they looked for the crumbs they found none. Little twittering birds which fly about in the woods and glades, had eaten them all, all up.

.   .   .   .   .

The two unhappy children walked all that night and the next day too, but the more they looked for the way, the more they lost it. They found nothing to eat but a few sour berries; and at last, weak and hungry, they sank down on a cushion of moss and fell asleep.

A LITTLE BIRD SAT THERE IN A TREE

It was now the third morning since they had left their home. They started to walk again, but they only got deeper and deeper into the wood.

They felt small and strange in the large, silent forest. The trees were so tall and the shade was so dense. Flowers could not grow in that dim, gloomy place—not even ferns. Only pale waxy mushrooms glowed faintly among the shadows, and weird lichens clung to the tree-trunks. Suddenly, into the vast green silence fell a ripple of sound so sweet, so gay, so silvery, that the children looked up in breathless wonder. A little white bird sat there in a tree; and when its beautiful song was ended, it spread its wings and fluttered away with anxious little chirps as though it wished to say, "Follow me! Follow me!"

Hansel and Gretel followed gladly enough, and all at once they found themselves in a fair flowery clearing, at the edge of which stood a tiny cottage.

The children stood hand in hand and gazed at it in wonder. "It's the loveliest house I ever saw," gasped Gretel, "and it looks good enough to eat."

They hurried on, and as they reached the little house,

12

"IT'S THE LOVELIEST HOUSE I EVER SAW," GASPED GRETEL

Hansel touched it and cried, "Gretel! It *is* good enough to eat."

And, if you can believe it, that's just what it was. Its walls were made of gingerbread, its roof was made of cake. It was trimmed with cookies and candy, and its window-panes were of pure transparent sugar. Nothing could have suited the children better and they began eating right away, they were so hungry! Hansel plucked a cookie from the roof and took a big bite out of it. Gretel munched big slabs of sugar-pane which she had broken from the window.

Suddenly a honeyed voice came floating from the house. It said:

> Nibble, nibble, nottage,
> Who's nibbling at my cottage?

To which the children said mischievously:

> It's only a breeze,
> Blowing down from the trees.

At this, the door burst open, and out slithered a bent old woman, waggling her head and leaning on a knotted stick. Hansel stopped munching his cookie and Gretel stopped crunching her sugar-pane. They were frightened—and no wonder! The Old One was far from beautiful. Her sharp nose bent down to meet her bristly chin. Her face, all folds and wrinkles, looked like an old shriveled pear; and she had only three teeth, two above and one below, all very long and yellow.

When the Old One saw that the children were turning to run away, she said in sugary tones, "Ei, ei! my little darlings, what has brought you here? Come right in and stay with me. I'll take good care of you."

She led them inside, and there in the middle of the room was a table neatly spread with toothsome dainties: milk, pancakes and honey, nuts, apples and pears.

While the children were eating their fill, the Old One made up two little beds which stood at one end of the room. She fluffed up the feather bed and puffed up the pillows, she turned back the lily-white linen, and then she said: "There, my little rabbits—a downy nest for each of you. Tumble in and slumber sweetly."

As soon as Hansel and Gretel were sound asleep, the Old One walked over and looked at them.

"Mm! Mm! Mm!" she said. "They're mine for certain!"

Now why should she do that? Well, I must tell you the real truth about the Old One. She wasn't as good and friendly as she pretended to be. She was a bad, bad witch who had built that sweet and sugary house on purpose to attract little children. Witches have ruby-red eyes and can hardly see at all, but oh! how they can smell with those long sharp noses of theirs! What they can

16

smell is human beings; and that morning, as Hansel and Gretel were wandering around in the forest, the Old One knew it well enough. Sniff! sniff! sniff! went her nose—she had been sniffing and waiting for them all day.

The next morning while the two little innocents were still sleeping peacefully, the Old One looked greedily at their round arms and rosy cheeks. "Mm! Mm! Mm!" she mumbled. "Juicy morsels!"

She yanked Hansel out of bed, dragged him into the back yard, and locked him up in the goose-coop. Hansel screamed and cried but it did him no good.

Then the Old One went into the house, gave Gretel a rough shake and cried, "Up with you, lazy bones. Make haste and cook some food for your brother. He's out in the goose-coop and if we feed him well, ei! ei! what a tasty boy he'll make!"

When Gretel heard this she burst into tears, but the Old One gave her a cuff on the ears and said, "Stop howling, you fool. Pick up your legs and do as I tell you."

Each day Gretel had to cook big pots full of fattening food for Hansel, and each morning the Old One hobbled out to the goose-coop and cried, "Hansel, let me see your finger so I can tell how fat you're getting."

But Hansel never showed her his finger. He always poked out a dry old bone, and the Old One, because of her red eyes, never knew the difference. She thought it really was his finger, and wondered why it was that he did not, did not get fat.

When four weeks had passed and Hansel seemed to stay thin, the Old One became impatient and said to Gretel, "Hey there, girl! Heat up a big kettle of water. I'm tired of waiting and, be he fat or lean, I'm going to have Hansel for my supper tonight."

18

Gretel cried and pleaded with her. But the Old One said, "All that howling won't do you a bit or a whit of good. You might as well spare your breath."

She built a roaring fire in the stove and said to Gretel, "First we'll do some baking. I've mixed and kneaded the dough, and the loaves are all ready for the oven." Then she opened the oven door and added in a sweet voice, "Do you think it's hot enough for the bread, Gretel dear? Just stick your head in the oven and see, there's a good girl!"

Gretel was about to obey, when a bird (the same white bird which had led them out of the forest) began to sing a song. It seemed to Gretel he was singing:

> Beware, beware,
> Don't look in there.

So Gretel didn't look into the oven. Instead she said to the Old One, "Well, I really don't know how to go about it. Couldn't you first show me how?"

"Stupid!" cried the Old One. "It's easy enough. Just stick your head way in and give a good look around. See? Like this!"

19

As the Old One poked her horrid old head into the oven, Gretel gave her a push and a shove, closed the oven door, bolted it swiftly and ran away. The Old One called and cried, and frizzled and fried, but no one heard. That was the end of her, and who cares?

Gretel was already in the back yard. "Hansel!" she cried. "We are free!" She opened the door of the goose-coop and out popped Hansel. The children threw their arms about each other and hopped and skipped around wildly.

But now there came a soft whirr in the air. The children stopped dancing and looked up. The good white bird and many others—all the twittering birds from the fields and glades—were flying through the air and settling on the cake-roof of the gingerbread house.

On the roof was a nest full of pearls and sparkling gems. Each little forest-bird took out a pearl or a gem and carried it down to the children. Hansel held out his hands, and Gretel held up her apron to catch all these treasures, while the little white bird sat on the roof and sang:

> Thank you for the crumbs of bread,
> Here are gems for you instead.

Now Hansel and Gretel understood that these were the very same birds who had eaten up their crumbs in the forest, and that this was how they wished to show their thanks.

As the birds fluttered away, Hansel said, "And now, little sister, we must make haste and get out of this witchy wood. As for me, I got very homesick sitting in that goose-coop week after week."

"And I," said Gretel. "Yes, I've been homesick too. But, Hansel, here we are so far from home, and how can we ever find our way back?"

Ho, what luck! There was the little white bird fluttering ahead of them once more. It led them away and soon they were in a green meadow. In front of them lay a big, big pond. How to get over it! As Hansel and Gretel stood on the shore wondering what to do, a

large swan came floating by, and the children said:

Float, swan, float!
Be our little boat.

The swan dipped its graceful head, raised it and dipped it again—that meant yes. When the swan had taken the children, one by one, to the other shore, they thanked it prettily and patted its long curved neck. Near the water's edge ran a neat little path. Hansel and Gretel followed it, and now the trees and the fields began to look familiar. Soon they saw their father's house gleaming through the trees and they ran home

as fast as they could. The father, who had been grieving and looking for his lost children all this time, was sitting in front of the hearth gazing sadly into the fire. As the door burst open and his two little ones ran in with shouts and laughter, his eyes filled with tears of joy. He hugged them and kissed them, and all he could say was: "My treasures, my little treasures!"

"Oh, as to treasures, papa," said Hansel, putting his hands into his pockets, "we'll show you some! See, now we will never have to starve again." At this, Gretel poured a shower of jewels from her apron, while Hansel added handful after handful from his pockets.

And the hard-hearted stepmother, where was she? Well, I'll tell you. When Hansel and Gretel seemed to be gone for good, the woman saw that her husband could think of nothing but his lost children. This made her so angry that she packed up her things in a large red handkerchief and ran away. She never came back, and Hansel and Gretel and their good father lived happily ever after.

CAT AND MOUSE
KEEP HOUSE

CAT AND MOUSE KEEP HOUSE

A TAWNY yellow cat with sea-green eyes, fine manners and a noble bearing, was taking an after-dinner stroll. What should he see but a mouse, a likable little mouse with handsome ears and big trusting eyes. The mouse was frightened and darted off but the cat called her back. Having just dined on two very plump mice, the cat did not feel like catching another, so he said, "Grey-mouse, my friend, somehow I like you well. Couldn't we be comrades and set up housekeeping together?"

The mouse, relieved at not being eaten on the spot, agreed gladly enough.

"Shall we not go house-hunting immediately?" said the cat.

Yes, the mouse thought they should. After looking at several cellars and barns, they found a quiet dark corner in a woodshed. It was clean, well-hidden and padded with straw.

"Now I've been thinking," said the cat. "We can find plenty of food while it's warm. But what about later? Shall we not buy ourselves a nice crock of lard against the winter?"

Yes, the mouse thought they should, so they bought a crock full of lard and took it home.

"Now we must hide it somewhere," said the cat. "But where? That is the question."

The mouse knew she could never think of a place, so she waited for the cat to speak. The cat did.

"I can think of no better place," said he, walking around and slowly lashing his tail, "no better place than the church. No one would steal in a church, you know. We'll tuck it away under the altar and we won't touch it, we won't even think of it, until it's very cold outdoors."

So they hid their crock of lard in the church, and the mouse thought no more about it. But as for the cat, he could think of nothing else, and one day he said: "What I was going to say, Grey-mouse—I've been asked to a christening at my cousin's house. She's just had a new baby, a right sweet little kitten, white with

brown spots. I'm to stand godfather to it; you wouldn't mind taking care of the house while I'm away, would you?"

No, the mouse didn't mind, and she wished the cat a very merry time besides.

Whether or not the cat really had a cousin I don't know, but he never went to a christening, that's certain. He went to the church, sneaked under the altar, and licked and licked at the crock of lard until the top layer was all off. Then, feeling very good inside, he took a little walk over some low housetops, admired the landscape, and finally stretched out for a comfortable nap in the sun. Whenever he thought of the good meal he had eaten, he licked his chops and wiped his whiskers, hoping to get just one more taste of it.

In the evening he returned to his home in the woodshed.

"Well, here you are again," said the mouse. "You must have had a gay day."

"Oh yes indeed," said the cat, closing his eyes and settling down for another snooze. "It came off very well."

"And what did they name the little baby?" asked the mouse.

"Top-off," said the cat, just like that.

"Top-off?" cried the mouse. "That's an odd name, to be sure. Is it a common one in your family?"

"What's the matter with that name?" said the cat, opening one eye. "It's as good a name as Crumb-snatcher—that's what *your* god child was called, wasn't it?"

The mouse couldn't deny this, so there was an end to the matter.

.   .   .   .   .

The cat could not forget how delicious the lard had tasted, so a few days later he said, "Grey-mouse, my friend, I must ask you to mind the house again today. I've been invited to stand godfather at another christening, and as the child is remarkably beautiful—silvery

grey with a white ring around its neck—I can hardly refuse. You don't mind, do you?"

No, the mouse didn't mind, and she wished the cat a very merry time besides.

The cat went back to the church, padded noiselessly along the aisle, and crept under the altar. The lard seemed to taste even better than before. He licked and licked until half the lard was out of the crock. He smacked his lips and as he sat down to wipe the last greasy drop from his paws, he said, "Nothing tastes so good as what one eats oneself!"

He went home, well pleased with his day's work, and when the mouse saw him, she said, "And what kind of a name did they give this baby?"

"Half-gone," said the cat.

"Half-gone?" cried the mouse. "Such a name I've never heard in all my life before. I'm sure you couldn't find it in the calendar."

"It seems to me a very good name," said the cat, purring softly at the thought of his recent feast. "And it's as good as the name of your sister, Cheese-filcher, whom you're always talking about."

This silenced the mouse and for several days nothing happened. The cat was trying to forget about the crock of lard but he couldn't. His mouth watered for another taste of it so he said to the mouse, "All good things come in threes, my friend, and now I am invited to another christening. The child is pure black except for its paws and whiskers, which are white as the driven snow. That sort of kitten is very rare and isn't born often. You can see I must go. You don't mind, do you?"

Well no, the mouse didn't exactly mind, but she said, "It seems to me that a great many kittens are being born into your family all of a sudden. And those odd names: Top-off, Half-gone—one can't help having queer thoughts about them."

"That comes from never getting out into the daylight," said the cat. "Who wouldn't have queer thoughts with the life you lead? Here you sit in a dark corner, day in and day out, fancying all sorts of foolish things."

The cat went off and made straight for the lard crock in the church. He licked and licked until the last greasy drop was gone. He gave a great sigh and said, "When all is eaten, then one has peace of mind at last."

It was after dark when he came home, looking very sleek and plump and innocent.

"Well, here you are at last," said the mouse. "And how did *this* christening go off?"

"Oh, everything came out fine," said the cat.

"And the new baby, what did they call him?" asked the mouse.

"Oh, you're sure not to like his name either," said the cat. "They called him All-gone."

"All-gone? You don't say!" cried the mouse. "I'm sure I've never seen that name in print anywhere." What could it mean? She shook her head in a puzzled way, curled herself into a little silver-grey ball, and went to sleep.

.   .   .   .   .

After that, for some reason, there were no more christenings in the cat's family. One day passed like the next for the rest of the summer and all through the autumn besides. But when the cold winds began to blow and the snow came falling down in big soft flakes, the mouse said: "Well, dear friend, a nip of lard now and then would help to keep us warm these chilly days. Our crock in the church—don't you think it's time we got it out?"

Yes, the cat thought it was, and they went off to the church together. The crock was still there but of course it was empty.

"Alas!" said the mouse, "now it all comes to light. What a fine friend you are, telling me all about those christening parties. I see the meaning of those odd names now: first Top-off, next Half-gone, and then . . ."

"Stop!" cried the cat. "Not one word more or you'll be sorry."

". . . All-gone." The words were already on the mouse's tongue and she could not stop herself. The cat gave a leap and a pounce, and the mouse was all gone too.

Oh dear, that's the way things go in this world!

SIX SERVANTS

SIX SERVANTS

IN days of yore there lived a Queen. She was old and ugly, but her daughter, who of course was a Princess, was young and charming. She was called the fairest maiden under the sun, and many a youth, hearing tales of her dazzling beauty, had traveled from afar to win her heart and hand.

All had failed, none had come back to tell the tale, and it was the ugly old Queen who was to blame for this.

The truth is, she was not only a Queen, but a witch as well! Her head was crammed with spells and harmful charms, her heart was filled with hate. Each day she lay in wait for the youths who came to ask for the hand of her Princess daughter.

Whenever one of these luckless lads appeared, the ugly old Witch-Queen would bob her head and say: "Very well. I'll set three tasks for you. If you fulfill them, my daughter is yours. If you fail, you must forfeit your life!" And of course she always made her problems so hard and impossible that no poor mortal had ever been able to solve a single one.

Now, in another castle in a land far, far away, there dwelt a young and handsome Prince. He was fearless and brave, and luck followed him everywhere like a faithful dog. When he heard of the dazzling Princess and her ugly old mother, he was fired with the desire to win the one and outwit the other.

40

"Please let me try!" he said to his father.

But the King replied, "Never! If you go, you are as good as dead. No one has escaped so far; what makes you think that you'll fare better? No, no, my boy, I cannot let you go."

Thereupon the Prince lay down in his bed and became gravely ill. For seven years he lay at death's door, and no doctor could help him. When the King saw that nothing could be done about it, he said sadly and with deep misgivings, "Try it then, my poor boy. I know no other way to help you."

As soon as the young Prince heard this, he rose from his bed, was hale and hearty once more, and looked radiantly happy. He called for his favorite steed, leaped into the saddle and galloped off. He wanted to try his luck all alone and did not even take a servant or a guard with him.

His way took him over a wide heath, and as he was riding along, he saw something in the distance which puzzled him. Was it a haystack? Was it a hill? He could not tell, but coming closer, he saw it was neither a hill nor a haystack. It was the big fat paunch of a

big fat man who lay there on his back and gazed lazily at the sky.

When The Fat One saw the Prince, he lifted himself up on his elbows and said, "I see you have no servant. In case you need one, you could take me."

Said the Prince: "True, I have no servant, but I really don't see how I could use such a monstrous big man as you are."

"Oh ho! This is nothing!" laughed The Fat One. "When I really spread myself out, I am three thousand times as big as I am now."

"Well, if that is the case," said the Prince, "I think I can use you. Come along."

. . . . .

The Fat One came, and the two traveled on. By and by they saw a pair of big feet stretched out on the ground. There were legs on the feet too, but they extended so far into the distance that it was impossible to see the full length of them. The Prince and The Fat One walked on, and now the calves, next the knees, then the thighs of those legs came into view. After a while they came to the man's body and at last they reached his head.

Said the Prince: "Well, well, my man, you're about as long as today and tomorrow."

"Oh, that's nothing," said The Long One. "When I really stretch myself out, I am three thousand times as

43

long as I am now. I have no master, could you use me?"

"I can use you," said the Prince. "Come along."

The Long One came, and soon the three travelers saw a man with a long thin neck. He was stretching it

out full length and was turning his head this way and that. From each of his eyes, which were clear as water, a long bright beam of light shone forth.

Said the Prince: "What are you looking at so eagerly?"

"Just looking around," said The Looker. "My eyes are so clear, there's nothing I can't see. I can see every forest and field, every hill and hollow, every place in the world."

"You are just the man I need," said the Prince. "If you care to be my servant, come along."

.   .   .   .   .

The Looker came, and all four traveled on until they saw a man who was crouching down with his ear to the ground.

Said the Prince: "What are you doing there?"

"Listening," said the man.

"Listening to what?" asked the Prince.

"Just listening to what's going on in the world. I've got very special ears—you see they're extra large—and there's nothing I can't hear. I can even hear the grass grow."

"If that's the case," said the Prince, "I can use you. If you want to be my servant, come along."

.   .   .   .   .

The Listener came, and all five traveled on until they saw a man with bandaged eyes.

46

Said the Prince: "My man, why are you blindfolded? Is it because your eyes are weak?"

"On the contrary," answered the man. "My eyes are very sharp and strong, and so whatever I look upon is shattered into a thousand pieces."

"I can use you, Shatter Eyes," said the Prince. "If you wish to be my servant, come along."

.   .   .   .   .

Shatter Eyes came, and all six traveled on until they saw a man hunched up by the roadside. He was smothered in shawls and mufflers, and although he was sitting in the hot noontide sun, he was shaking and shivering, and his teeth were chattering and clattering.

Said the Prince: "My poor man! On such a hot day what makes you so cold?"

"It's the heat makes me so c-cold," chattered the man. "I'm a curious fellow and not like other folk. The h-hotter it is, the frostier I get, and the f-frostier it is, the hotter I get. In the midst of cold, I sweat and swelter; in the midst of heat, I sh-shiver and sh-shake. Brrr!"

"You are indeed a strange fellow," said the Prince.

47

"I am sure you would come in handy some time. If you want to be my servant, Frosty-hot, come along."

Frosty-hot came, and the Prince was much pleased with his six new servants.

They all traveled on. The Prince led the way and each in turn followed him: The Fat One and The Long One, The Looker and The Listener, Shatter Eyes and Frosty-hot.

.   .   .   .   .

When they reached the Witch-Queen's country, the Prince left his six servants at an inn and went alone to the Queen's castle. He did not tell her who he was, but merely said: "You have a beautiful Princess daughter. I intend to win and wed her, and am ready for any task you may set me."

The Witch-Queen was delighted at getting such a handsome youth in her clutches.

"Fine! Fine!" she said. "Take your chance, my boy, take your chance. I will set three tasks for you. If you fulfill them, you can have the girl. If you fail—well, that's the end of you, my lad!" She was smirking and rubbing her hands—it was easy to see she could hardly wait for him to fail.

"I am ready," said the Prince. "What is the first task?"

"Heh! Heh!" cackled the Witch-Queen. "In the bottom of the Red Sea lies a ring. I must have it by noon today."

The Prince walked off with a jaunty step, but he

did not feel as carefree as he looked. When he reached the inn he said to his six servants, "The first task is certainly not an easy one. Old Ugly-face wants a ring which lies at the bottom of the Red Sea and says she must have it by noon today. Can any of you help me to find it?"

"Let me look!" said The Looker. He stretched out his neck, turned his head this way and that, and took a long, long look. The beams from his eyes shone forth, far, far, far out into the world, and down, down, down to the bottom of the Red Sea.

"I see the ring!" he cried. "It's hanging on the tip

of a jagged rock in the very middle of the water, but how can we reach it?"

Now The Long One lifted them all on his back. Then, with a few big strides, he walked to the shore of the Red Sea and said, "Well, here I am. I could reach it easily enough, but there's so much water I can't see the stone. Now, what can we do about that?"

"Oh well, I can do something about that!" laughed The Fat One. He puffed himself up until he was three thousand times as fat as he was before. Then he lay down on the shore, placed his lips to the water's edge, and drank and drank and drank. One wave after another disappeared, and at last he had swallowed up the whole Red Sea—and there, sure enough, was a jagged stone on which dangled a ring.

The Long One leaned over, grabbed the ring, and handed it to the Prince.

The Prince was overjoyed and hurried to the Witch-Queen's castle without delay. When the old Queen saw the ring she was almost too astonished to speak, but at last she managed to say, "Yes, it's the right ring, there's no doubt about that. But of course the first task is always easy. The second will be harder."

"I am ready," said the Prince. "What is it?"

"Heh! Heh!" cackled the Queen. "In my big meadow are three hundred plump oxen. By sundown tonight every ox must be eaten up—hair, hide, hooves and horns. Also in my cellar are three hundred casks of wine. This wine must be drunk up to the last drop, and by sunset, too. See what you can do about that!"

"And may I not invite some guests to this marvelous feast?" asked the Prince. "After all, no meal tastes good without company."

"Oh well," said the Queen with a malicious laugh, "you may invite *one,* but that's all. Heh! Heh! Heh!"

The Prince walked off, whistling loudly, and when he reached the inn he said to The Fat One, "Come, my dear fellow. I'm afraid you haven't been getting enough to eat, but today you shall be my guest at a feast which you will not soon forget."

When The Fat One saw the three hundred plump oxen and the three hundred casks of wine, he puffed himself out and out and out, until he was three thousand times as fat as he had been. Then he gobbled up the three hundred oxen so that neither hair, hide, hooves nor horns were left, and said, "Well, that was a good breakfast." Then he drank the wine out of the three hundred casks without leaving a single drop. When this mighty feast was finished, he felt fine, wobbled back to the inn and fell into a contented sleep.

52

The Prince went to the Witch-Queen and when he told her the second task was fully completed, she was even more astonished than the first time. But she did not show it, and with a false smile she said, "You are indeed a remarkable lad. And now, are you ready for the third task?"

"I am ready," said the Prince. "What is it?"

"Heh! Heh!" cackled the Queen. "Tonight you must sit beside my daughter and put your arm around her. Take care that you don't fall asleep and that she doesn't get away from you. At midnight I'll appear, and if she isn't there in your arms, it's all over with you."

"That's easy," thought the Prince. "All I have to do is to keep my eyes open and hold her tight."

But as he thought it over he said to himself, "No, it sounds too easy; there must be a catch in it. And in order to be on the safe side, I'll get my six servants to keep strict watch tonight."

At dusk the ugly old Queen brought her dazzling daughter to the Prince's quarters at the inn. She directed the handsome young pair to sit side by side on a bench and then she placed the young lad's arm about the

maiden's shoulder. This done, she left, cackling softly to herself.

After the old Queen was well out of sight, The Long One twined himself round and round the bench so that the Princess could not get away, The Fat One planted himself before the door so that no one could get in, and the other four servants sat together nearby, all ready for action in case they were needed.

Well, well—the hours wore on and there sat the handsome Prince beside the dazzling Princess. The girl looked sweetly contented, and as for the Prince, he could not keep his eyes off such an entrancing vision. He was happy beyond words and did not feel the least bit sleepy.

This pleasant situation might have continued all night, but such was not the Queen's plan. At eleven o'clock she threw an enchantment over them all. In a twinkling everything was changed. The Prince was fast asleep. So was The Fat One at the door. So was The Long One, twined around the bench. So were The Looker, The Listener, Shatter Eyes and Frosty-hot.

But the Witch-Queen, too sure of her success, had not made the spell strong enough, and at a quarter of twelve the enchantment wore off. The Prince was the first to open his eyes. His arm was no longer around the Princess, for the Princess was—gone!

"Alas! Alas!" cried the Prince. "Now I am lost forever!"

At this the six servants woke up and they too began to weep and wail and wring their hands.

Suddenly:

"Hush! Hush!" whispered The Listener, cupping his hand to his huge ear, "I hear something! It's the voice of the Princess, I think. She's crying. What is it she is saying? Something about being in a rock. Take a look, Looker. Maybe you can see her."

The Looker stretched his neck and took a long, long look. It was a look one hundred miles long. He couldn't see her. Then he took a long, long and longer look— this was a look two hundred miles long. Still he couldn't see her. At last he took a long, long, long, and yet longer look—and this was a look three hundred miles long! The bright beams shone from his eyes: first to the East, next to the South, now to the West, and then to the North.

"I see her!" he cried at last. "She's in a rock, sure enough, and it's three hundred miles due North. Shake a leg, Long One."

"Gladly," said The Long One. "But I'll need a helper. You, Shatter Eyes, come along and off we'll go!"

The Long One bent down and lifted Shatter Eyes on his right shoulder. Then he stretched and stretched and stretched himself out until he was three thousand times as long as he had been. He strode due North and in a trice they were standing in front of the rock.

Shatter Eyes raised his bandage for just *one* second, and as his sharp glance smote the rock it burst into a thousand pieces—and there sat the Princess quite unharmed. She seemed much pleased at being rescued and stopped crying immediately.

The Long One bent down and lifted the Princess up on his left shoulder, and in three mighty strides, Left! Right! Left! all three were back at the inn.

Well, well! There they all sat once more, looking very cheerful and triumphant; the Prince with his arm around the Princess, and the six servants glaring around fiercely and keeping terrific guard.

At the stroke of midnight, the Witch-Queen came slinking in. She thought, of course, that her daughter was still bewitched and safely hidden in the rock three hundred miles away. On her face was a hideous grin and she was cackling softly to herself, "Now I've got him! Heh! Heh! Heh! Now I've got him!"

But when she saw the Prince, wide awake and with his arm around the Princess as though nothing had happened, she was so angry that she gave a loud hiss. The Prince had fulfilled the three tasks she had set him but she was not yet ready to give up. Horrid schemes grew in her head like weeds in a garden, and she soon thought of a way out.

Her power over the Prince was gone—she knew that —but her daughter was still under her power, so this is what she did:

She whispered something into her daughter's ear: "Swss! Swss! Swss! Swss! Tell him . . . Swss! Swss! Swss! Swss!"

What could the poor Princess do? She was under her mother's power and had to follow her command. So, although she hardly knew what she was saying, the Princess said to the Prince, "It is true you have won my hand. But the bargain was made without my consent. Have *I* nothing to say about it?"

The Prince, who always tried to be fair, said, "You

are right, dear Princess. Your consent has not been asked. What can I do to gain it?"

Now the Witch-Queen again leaned over and whispered into her daughter's ear: "Tell him . . . Swss! Swss! Swss!" And the poor Princess had to say to the Prince, "A big bonfire will be built here immediately. If you can find some one who will sit in the middle of it, I will marry you."

That was all the Witch-Queen's idea, of course. She thought no one would risk his life for the Prince, and so the Prince, to prove his love for the Princess, would have to sit in the bonfire himself. And that, thought the old Witch-Queen, would be fine, for then she would be rid of him forever.

But what she didn't know was that the Prince's faithful servants were already making plans to help him. They were talking among themselves, and they said: "We have all done something for our master, all but Frosty-hot. Come on, old fellow, it's your turn now."

They led him to the fire which was already blazing away; and Frosty-hot, drawing his shawls and mufflers about him, jumped in.

It was an enormous fire. Three hundred loads of wood were in it and it made a great heat for miles around. It burned for three days and three nights; and when

the last flames had died down, there among the ashes and cinders stood poor Frosty-hot, shaking and shivering. His teeth were chattering so that he could hardly talk, but at last he managed to stammer out: "S-s-such a f-frost I have never f-felt. Had it lasted l-longer, I'd have f-frozen to d-death!"

60

This was too much for the Witch-Queen. She saw it was all over with her and she took to her heels. But at that moment, Shatter Eyes lifted his bandage for just *one* second, and as his sharp glance struck her, she burst into a thousand pieces and that was the end of the wicked creature.

Every one breathed a sigh of relief, and even the Princess felt better. She was tired of being bewitched all the time, and now that she was her real self, she fell in love with the Prince then and there, and they lived in peace and happiness ever after.

SPINDLE, SHUTTLE AND NEEDLE

SPINDLE, SHUTTLE AND NEEDLE

AT the edge of a village lived an orphan girl and her godmother. They were poor and lived in a tiny cottage, where they made a modest living by spinning, weaving and sewing. The godmother was no longer young and as the years flowed on, she became too old to work. At last she was even too old to live any longer, so she called the girl to her bedside and said: "Little treasure, I must go. I have no money to leave you, but you have our little cottage which will shield you from the wind and stormy weather.

And you have also the spindle, the shuttle and the needle. These will always be your friends, and will help you to earn your bread and butter."

After that the girl lived all alone in the cottage. She went on with her work as before and although she never became rich, she managed to keep poverty from her door.

Now it happened that at this time a charming Prince was roaming through the land in search of a bride. His father, the King, would not let him marry a poor girl, and as for the Prince himself, he did not care for rich girls. Said he: "If I can find one who is both the poorest and the richest—that maiden shall be my Princess."

He soon became somewhat discouraged, for this combination was hard to find. Still he didn't give up, but wandered on and on. When he reached the village in which lived our little orphan girl, he asked, as he always did, who was the richest and poorest in that place. The villagers told him the name of the richest maiden—a proud haughty girl of high degree—and the poorest, said they, was an orphan lass who lived at the farthest edge of the village.

As soon as the rich girl heard that a charming Prince had arrived, she waited for him at her door, dressed in her Sunday best. When she saw him coming, she walked toward him with mincing steps, and dropped him a deep curtsy.

The Prince glanced at her and rode on without a word.

"She's a beauty and she may be rich," he said to himself, "but she's not rich *and* poor. No, she won't do."

When he reached the tiny cottage at the farthest edge of the village, the little orphan lass was nowhere in sight. The Prince drew up his horse and looked in through the open window. There in the bright morning sunshine sat the girl spinning, spinning, spinning away. At last she happened to glance up from her work and when she saw the kind handsome face at her window, she blushed a rosy red, lowered her eyes, and went on spinning as though her young life depended on it. She was so flustered she hardly knew whether the thread was running evenly or not. She was too shy to look up again, so she spun on and on until the Prince had ridden away. Then she tiptoed to the window and gazed after him until the jaunty white plume in his hat was no more than a blur in the blue distance.

When she sat down to spin again, she felt strangely happy. Her heart was dancing and, without knowing it,

67

she began to sing a little song which her good godmother had taught her long ago:

> Spindle, spindle, dance and roam;
> Lead my lover to my home.

To her surprise the spindle obeyed! It sprang out of her hand, out of the door. As the girl jumped up and looked after it in wonder, she saw it dancing merrily over the meadow, trailing a shimmery golden thread after it as it went. Then it disappeared into the blue distance; she could see it no longer.

That was the end of the spinning, so she took her shuttle and started to weave instead.

In the meantime the spindle was dancing and prancing after the unsuspecting Prince and at last it caught up with him. The Prince gazed at it in amazement.

"What do I see?" he cried. "Can it be that the spindle wants to lead me somewhere? I will follow its thread and see what happens."

He turned his horse around and followed the thread back.

Of course the girl knew nothing about all this. She was sitting at her work, weaving busily. She still felt gay and

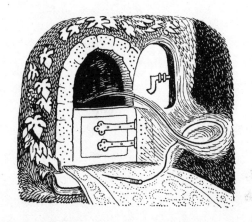

light at heart, she knew not why, and found herself singing
the second part of the old song her good godmother had
taught her:

> Shuttle, shuttle, weave away;
> Lead my lover back this day.

Suddenly the shuttle sprang out of her fingers and flew
away, but so quickly that the girl could not see where it had
gone. It darted out through the door and dropped upon
the doorstep where, all by itself, it began to weave a long
narrow carpet. It was a marvelously beautiful one. On
each side was a border of roses and lilies. Down the center,
on a golden ground, was a pattern of green vines with
rabbits darting here and there, deer peeping wide-eyed

through the leaves, and brilliant birds perching on the branches. Those birds, they looked so natural and gay, one almost expected them to sing; and everything looked as though it were growing by itself.

Back and forth leaped the shuttle, weaving wonders as it went, and all the time the carpet grew longer and longer.

The girl knew nothing of this. She thought her shuttle was lost so she sat down and began to sew instead. She still felt strangely happy and there was a song in her heart. Without realizing it, she sang it out loud:

> Needle, needle, sharp and fine;
> Tidy up this house of mine.

At that moment the needle sprang out of her fingers and flew about the room, here and there, in and out, back and forth. It was just as though fairy fingers were at work for, before the girl's astonished eyes, things were changing like magic. Rich green covers appeared from nowhere and flung themselves over table, bench and bed; filmy curtains hung themselves airily over the windows; the chairs were suddenly soft and plushy, and a rich glowy-red rug rolled itself out over the bare floor.

IT WAS JUST AS THOUGH FAIRY FINGERS WERE AT WORK

The girl was so entranced she could do nothing but look on, wide-eyed and wondering. Hardly had the needle finished its final stitch, when the girl spied something through the window which made her heart thump. It was a faint white blur in the distance. It was bobbing up and down and was coming nearer and becoming clearer every minute. It was the Prince, being led by the shimmery thread to her very gate. He leaped from his horse and was now walking on the marvelous carpet—where that had come from, the girl could not tell; for the shuttle, having accomplished its masterpiece, now lay modestly beside the door step. When the Prince reached the door he was enchanted by what he saw. The young girl was standing there in her plain little dress, but everything about her glowed like a rose in a bush. He held out his hand to her, saying, "At last I have found you! Yes, you are poor but you are also rich—rich in many things. Come with me, my dear, for you are to be my little Princess!"

The girl blushed a rosy red. She said not a word but she held out her little hand, and she was very happy. The Prince took her with him to his father's castle and made her his little Princess.

SPINDLE, SHUTTLE AND NEEDLE

But her good friends, the spindle, the shuttle and the needle—what became of them? They were not left behind, but were given a place in the royal treasure chamber. Many a mortal came to see the spindle which had lured the Prince back, the shuttle which had led him to the door, and the needle which had made a palace out of a poor girl's home.

DOCTOR KNOW-IT-ALL

DOCTOR KNOW-IT-ALL

Once there was a peasant and he was very poor. All he had in the world was a patch of woodland, a two-wheeled cart and a pair of oxen to pull it. From time to time he chopped down some of his trees, cut them up into logs and carted them into the village. If he was lucky enough to find a buyer, he would sell the wood for two dollars a load.

One day this peasant Fish (for that was his name) took his ox-cart full of wood to the village and sold it to a doctor. While Fish was standing at the open door waiting for his two dollars, a powerful smell of rich savory food reached his nostrils. Fish peeped in at the door. There was the doctor's dinner laid out on the table, all steaming and ready to eat: soup and roast, juicy vegetables, a frosted cake, and a dish of such luscious fruit as poor peasant Fish had never even laid eyes upon.

"Oh!" thought the poor man. "If I could only be a doctor too, and eat such heavenly dinners."

This set him thinking. After the doctor had given him the two dollars, the peasant lingered in the doorway, twirling his cap this way and that; and at last he asked whether he might not learn to be a doctor too.

"Why not?" said the doctor. "It's easy enough."

"And how would one go about that, now?" asked Fish.

"First of all," said the doctor, "you must sell your two oxen and the cart. With that money you must buy some fine clothes; also a few medicine bottles, pills and pellets, salts, salves and so on. Next you must get yourself a book—one of those A B C books will do, the kind with

a rooster inside. And last of all, you must get a board with the words I AM DOCTOR KNOW-IT-ALL painted on it, and this you must nail over your door."

Fish did all this. Over his door hung the newly painted sign, in his room was a shelf full of medicine bottles, on his table was the A B C book, while he himself was so fine and grand he felt like someone new. With his spectacles, his long-tailed coat, his watch and pointed beard, he really looked as though he knew it all. He was ready to start, but day after day went by and nothing happened. There he sat among his salves and pills with not a thing to do.

At last someone came, and a lord no less. This lord had been robbed of a big sum of money, and when he saw the sign, I AM DOCTOR KNOW-IT-ALL, he said to himself, "That's just the fellow I want. If he really knows it all, he will surely know who has stolen my money."

He knocked at the door, and when Fish heard him he straightened his spectacles, gave a pull at his watch chain, put on his tall hat but took it off again, and at last he opened the door.

"So you are Doctor Know-It-All," said the rich lord.

"Oh yes," said Fish.

"I want you to find my stolen money," said the lord. "Can you come with me now to my palace?"

"Yes indeed," said Fish, "and my wife, Gretl—can she come too?"

"Certainly," said the lord; so they all stepped into his coach and drove off.

It was the dinner hour when they reached the lord's palace, so he invited Fish and Gretl to join him. They all sat down at the table, and when the first servant came in with a dish of soup, Fish whispered to his wife, "Look, Gretl, that is the first."

He meant that this was the first course being served, but the servant, who had overheard him, thought he meant this was the first thief who had stolen the lord's money. As he really was one of the thieves he became worried, and when he reached the kitchen he said to the other servants, "Things will go ill with us, now that this Doctor Know-It-All is around here. Just think! As soon as he set eyes on me, he told his wife I was the first thief."

The other servants gasped in alarm, and when the bell tinkled for the next course, the second servant hardly had the courage to go into the dining room. But what could he do? It was his turn to serve. He tried to look innocent as he entered with a dish of steaming food, but Fish leaned over to his wife and whispered, "See, Gretl, that's the second."

He meant this was the second course but the servant thought that he himself was meant, and his knees knocked together as he rushed back to the kitchen.

When the third servant came in with still another dish,

it was the same. Fish nudged his wife, whispering, "And that, Gretl, is the third."

The third servant, his hair standing on end, set the dish on the table and dashed into the kitchen as fast as he could. Luckily the lord had noticed nothing. He had been too busy thinking up some way of putting Doctor Know-It-All to the test, and now he said, "Doctor, here is the fourth servant with a covered dish. If you really know it all, you should be able to guess what is in the dish."

Poor peasant Fish! How should he know what was in it? He looked and looked at the covered dish; and at last, seeing he was caught, he said, "Oh, you poor Fish. You're done for!"

As luck would have it, there was a fish in the dish, and now the lord cried, "Well, well, Doctor, you've guessed it! Now I know you can find my stolen money too."

Poor peasant Fish! He was in a fix and no mistake about it. He was still racking his brains for something to say, when the fourth servant, who was just leaving the room, winked meaningly at him. Fish excused himself from the table and followed the servant into the kitchen. The servants, looking greatly frightened, said: "Oh Doctor, you told your wife we were the thieves who stole milord's money, and it's true. But we'll give it all back to him and we'll reward you besides, if you'll only promise not to tell on us."

Fish promised to keep their secret, and they showed him where the stolen money was hidden. When he returned to the dining room he cleared his throat and stroked his beard, saying, "Hm, hm! So you want to know what's become of your money, milord. Hm, hm! Well, well! I'll have to consult my book about that."

He sat down and spread the A B C book on his knees. Then he put his spectacles on his nose; and, with an important air, he began to look for the picture of the rooster. Meanwhile the servants were curious to know whether the Doctor would really keep their secret, so the fifth servant was sent in to listen. He sneaked in on tiptoe and hid in the oven.

All this time, peasant Fish or Doctor Know-It-All (whichever you wish to call him) was still paging back and forth in his A B C book, but he couldn't find the picture of the rooster. At last he lost his temper and shouted,

"You rascal! I know you're in there and I'll find you yet."

The servant who was in hiding thought that he was meant. He jumped out of the oven, yelling, "Hulla! The man knows everything!"

Doctor Know-It-All, who had found the rooster at last, looked pleased, closed his A B C book and cleared his throat again.

"Hm, hm!" he said. "Yes. Well, well! And now as to your stolen money, milord. I can show you just where it is."

He led the lord to the place where the servants had hidden the money, saying, "You see, milord. Here it is, every penny of it."

The lord was pleased—so pleased, in fact, that he grabbed a big handful of gold, pressed it into Fish's hands and said, "Well done, my good Doctor, and my undying thanks to you. I will spread your fame far and wide."

This he did, too; and from that time on, Fish and his good wife Gretl lived in wealth and ease, had plenty of good food to eat, and rode about in a fine carriage.

THE MUSICIANS OF
BREMEN

THE MUSICIANS OF BREMEN

An old, old donkey, who had carried many a heavy load in his day, was now worn out and weary and could work no more. One day his master began making preparations to get him out of the way in order to save the cost of feeding him, but the donkey twitched his long ears and thought: "Something is up—I can feel it in the air. I had better get out of here while I can still use my legs."

So he sneaked out of the barn and, taking the path between his four feet, he made off for the town of Bremen, thinking he might join a band of street musicians there and so make a living for himself.

He had not gone very far when he came upon something lying in his path. It was a big hunting dog, who was panting as though he had run himself out of his last breath.

"Ei, big dog," said the donkey, "why are you panting so hard?"

"Oh! oh!" said the big dog, between gasps. "For many years I have been faithful to my master; tirelessly I guarded his home and helped him in the hunt. But now when I am old, half blind and deaf, and stiff of joint besides, my master does not want to feed me any more. Instead he plans to kill me, and so to save my hide, I took to my heels and here I am. But what good does it do me, after all? I am too old to earn my bread and meat and will surely starve by the wayside."

"Good friend," said the donkey, "my case was much the same as yours, and do you know what I am going to do? I am bound for Bremen-town, and there I plan to become a musician. Why don't you come with me and take up music too? I will play the lute and you can pound the kettle-drum—that will make a fine music, hei? And the people will surely throw us a few pennies for it."

The dog was well pleased with this plan and the two runaways traveled on.

Before long they met a cat. She was sitting by the roadside, with a face as long as a three days' drizzle.

"Ei, ei, old Whisker-wiper!" said the donkey. "What's wrong with you?"

"Who can be cheerful when one's life is at stake?" said the cat. "For years I caught every rat and mouse in my master's house. But now that my eyes are dull and my teeth are blunt, I find it easier to sit by the fire and purr, than to shake a stiff leg and sniff around after mice. So now my mistress doesn't need me any more, and this morning she wanted to drown me. But old as I am, I still have one of my nine lives left, and this I would dearly love to live out in some warm and cozy ingle-nook. And so, my friends, I picked up my old legs and ran away. But now that I'm here, where can I go and what can I do?"

"We two," said the donkey, "the dog and I—we are off to Bremen-town to become musicians. Wouldn't you like to join us? You surely have had much practice in the art of serenading—you won't even have to take lessons!"

The old cat, pleased with the compliment, came willingly enough, and so the three runaways traveled on.

Soon they came to a farm yard, and there on the gate post sat a ragged old rooster crowing away at the top of his lungs.

"Ei, Red-comb!" said the donkey. "Your screams are enough to pierce one's very marrow. What's up? What's up?"

"I've just been prophesying good weather for Lady Day," said the rooster, "so you see I'm still good for something. But just because I'm not as young as I used to be, my mistress wants to serve me up for Sunday dinner tomorrow. Tonight, my friends! tonight I am to lose my head; so I thought I might as well crow as long as that head is still on my shoulders."

"Ei, ei, Red-comb!" said the donkey. "There's no need to let yourself be snuffed out like that. In any case you would do better to come with us; we're all off to Bremen-town to become musicians. You have a fine lusty voice— when we're all making music together and you put in a loud *keekerikee* here and there—hei! that will be something to listen to!"

90

The rooster was delighted at being able to crow for many a day more, and so the four runaways traveled on.

But the town of Bremen was far away; the four travelers could not reach it in one day. Towards nightfall they found themselves in the middle of a forest and they decided to spend the night there. The donkey and the dog lay down under a big tree, while the cat and the rooster made themselves comfortable up above; the cat on the lower branches, and the rooster on the topmost twig, as this was the safest place for him. But before he closed his eyes, our rooster took a long look around the country-side. From his tree-top perch he could see far and wide and as he looked he saw, not very far away, a tiny light glimmering among the trees.

"Hey! Hey!" he called down to his companions. "There must be a house near by. I see a light!"

"Oh yes?" said the donkey. "Then we must get up and go there. Our quarters here are none too comfortable."

The others agreed, the dog adding that a few bones with a little meat on them would do him much good, while the cat thought a saucer full of milk would not come amiss. So the four travelers made their way toward the light. The little glimmer became bigger and bigger, and at last they found themselves in front of a brightly-lighted robbers' den! The donkey, being the tallest, crept up to the window and looked in.

"What do you see, Long-ears?" whispered the rooster.

"What do I see?" said the donkey. "A table laden with food and drink, and a band of robbers sitting there, taking their fill of it."

"Ah! That would be something for us now!" said the dog.

"Yes, yes," said the donkey. "If it were only we, instead, who were sitting there!"

This idea worked so strongly on their minds, that they decided they must find a way to get rid of the robbers and sit in their places at the table. At last they thought of a plan and it did not take them long to carry it out. The donkey stood at the window with his fore feet on the ledge, the dog jumped on the donkey's back, the cat climbed on the dog's back, while the rooster flew up and perched himself on top of the cat.

This done, they waited for the donkey's signal, at which they started off to make their music, all together and as

THEY WAITED FOR THE DONKEY'S SIGNAL

loud as they could. The donkey brayed, the dog barked, the cat meowed, and the rooster crowed *keekerikee!* In the middle of this concert, all four plunged through the window with a crash and clatter and a wild splintering of glass. The robbers jumped up, pale with fear and horror. They were sure a pack of demons was bursting in upon them so they fled, terror-stricken, into the heart of the forest, where they huddled together with pounding hearts and shaking knees.

Our four musicians, however, lost no time in making themselves at home. They sat down at the table, were well content to take what the robbers had left, and ate as though a four weeks' fast were ahead of them.

When they had eaten their fill, they blew out the light, and found their places for the night; each after his nature and according to his own idea of comfort. The donkey went outdoors and lay down on top of the manure heap. The dog stretched himself under the kitchen table beside the door. The cat sat on the hearth beside the warm ashes, and Red-comb found a fine roost on the gable of the house. They were all very tired after their long day's tramp, and soon they were fast asleep.

Some time after midnight, the robbers came forth from their hiding place, and began to look around. When they saw from afar that there were no lights in their den, they walked a little closer. All seemed safe and silent, and the robber chief said, "What fools we were to let ourselves get so frightened over a little noise!"

He ordered one of the robbers to go to the house and look around. The robber did as he was told and, finding everything very peaceful and quiet, he decided to go into the kitchen and light a lamp. On the hearth the cat's eyes were glowing in the darkness, but the robber thought they were smoldering embers and he held out his match to kindle it. But the cat would stand no nonsense, and she sprang at him, spitting and scratching. The robber was frightened out of his wits and made for the kitchen-door, but the dog, who lay there, leaped up and bit him in the leg. The robber screamed and ran out of the door as fast as he could, but as he passed the manure heap, the donkey gave him a hearty kick with his hind hoof. And now the rooster, who had been awakened by all this din, thought it was morning, and cried, "Keekerikee! Keekerikee!"

The robber's heels did not stop flying until he reached

his robber chief once more. He was puffing and panting and his trembling knees could hardly hold him up.

"What horrors!" he gasped. "In the house, by the fire, sits a fiendish witch; she breathed her hot breath on me and scratched my face with her long finger nails. In front of the kitchen door lies a man with a knife; he stabbed my leg as I passed by. Out in the barn-yard lurks a black monster; he gave me a whack with a heavy club. Up on the roof sits a judge, and as I ran by he screamed: 'See the thief flee! See the thief flee!' Well, that was too much. I took to my heels and here I am, and I'll never go back there again!"

He didn't, nor did the rest of the robbers, nor did their chief, for now they were sure that their den was inhabited by ghosts and demons.

THE MUSICIANS OF BREMEN

As to our brave musicians—they never went to Bremen-town at all. They were so satisfied with their new home they saw no reason for going any farther; and all four, who had once been so close to losing their lives, lived out the days of their old age in ease and comfort.

CINDERELLA

CINDERELLA

A RICH man had lost his wife and was left all alone with his little girl. Although they were lonely and sad, father and daughter lived together peacefully enough through the summer, the autumn, and the winter. But when spring came, the man married again, and from that time on, all was different for the little girl.

When the new wife arrived she brought two daughters of her own. These were as homely as they were haughty, and when they saw that the little girl outshone them in beauty, they took a great dislike to her and decided to get her out of the way.

"Why should the little fool be allowed to sit in the parlor with us?" said they. "If she wants food, let her work for it. All she's fit for is the kitchen. Out with her!"

They took away her pretty clothes and dressed her in

drab rags and clumsy shoes. They shoved her into the kitchen and made her work very hard. She had to get up at dawn, build the fire, carry the water, and take care of the cooking and washing besides. And that wasn't all. At night, after a hard day's work, the poor little thing had not even a bed to sleep in! The only way she could keep warm was to lie on the hearth among the ashes and cinders, and because of this she was now called Cinderella.

.   .   .   .   .

Now it happened one day that the father decided to go to the fair, so he asked his two step-daughters what they would like to have him bring home for them.

"Beautiful dresses," said one.

"Jewels," said the other.

"And you, Cinderella?" asked the father. "What would you like to have?"

"Please bring me a fresh green hazel twig, papa—the first one which brushes your hat on the way home."

At the fair the man bought rich gowns and sparkling jewels for his two step-daughters, and as he was riding home along a narrow woodland road, a little green hazel twig snapped against his hat and pushed it off.

"Well, well, I almost forgot!" said the father as he broke off the twig. "That's what little Cinderella asked for."

The two step-sisters were delighted with their gorgeous presents and were soon prancing before their mirrors, primping and preening themselves like the vain creatures they were. Cinderella was pleased, too, with her simple present. She took the hazel twig and planted it in the garden behind the house. She watered it every day: it grew and grew, and soon it was a little tree.

One day a dove came and made its home in the tree. It fluttered among the leafy branches, perched on the little twigs, and cooed softly. Cinderella loved the dove, for it was the only friend she had. She gave it crumbs and seeds, and the dove was grateful and sang: "Rookety goo, rookety goo."

·　　·　　·　　·　　·

One day there came news of a big party to be given at the royal palace. It was to last three days and nights and the King had invited all the young ladies in the kingdom, so that his son, a young and handsome Prince, might choose one of them for his future bride.

What a flurry there was in every household! All the maidens in the land were full of hope and excitement, and none more so than Cinderella's haughty step-sisters. They were determined to dazzle the Prince at all costs and were in a fever of preparation for weeks before the event.

At last the first day of the festival arrived and the two sisters began dressing for the big ball. It took them all afternoon, and when they had finished, they were worth looking at.

They were dressed in satin and silk. Their bustles were puffed, their bodices stuffed, their skirts were ruffled and tufted with bows; their sleeves were muffled with furbelows. They wore bells that tinkled, and glittering rings; and rubies and pearls and little birds' wings! They plastered their pimples and covered their scars with moons and stars and hearts. They powdered their hair, and piled it high with plumes and jeweled darts.

At the last minute Cinderella was called in to curl their hair, lace up their bodices and dust off their shoes. When the poor little girl heard they were going to a party at the

THEY WENT RUSTLING AND TINKLING TO THE BALL

King's palace, her eyes sparkled and she asked her step-mother whether she might not go too.

"You?" cried the step-mother. "You, all dusty and cindery, want to go to a party? You haven't even a dress to wear and you can't dance."

But Cinderella begged and begged until the step-mother, in order to get rid of her, said: "Very well, I'll tell you what I'll do. I'll toss a panful of peas into the ashes, and if you can pick out all the good ones and get them back into the pan in two hours, you may go."

Cinderella knew she could never do all this alone, but she knew what no one else did—and what was that? She knew that her hazel tree had magic in it and that her little dove was a fairy dove. So she went out under the hazel tree and said softly:

> Fairy dove-friend in the tree,
> Birds that fly
> In the sky,
> Come and help me!

The dove replied:

> Rookety goo!
> What can we do?

And Cinderella said:

> The good peas in the pan
> As fast as you can.
> Please help me!

Down flew the dove, and down flew all the birds in the sky, and up and down went all their little heads as they picked up the peas.

"Pick, peck! Pick, peck!" went the birds, and soon every good pea was out of the ashes and back in the pan. The birds flew away and Cinderella hurried off to show the pan full of peas to her step-mother.

When she saw this, the step-mother was astonished and angry, and she said crossly, "All the same, you can't go. You have no dress, and you can't dance with those clumsy feet of yours."

Tears rolled down Cinderella's cheeks, and she begged and begged until her step-mother said, "Very well, I'll give you another chance. This time you'll have to clean two pans full of peas and I'll give you only one hour to do it in." And she walked off, muttering, "That ought to keep her busy until we're well on our way."

Again Cinderella stood under her hazel tree and said softly:

> Fairy dove-friend in the tree,
>   Birds that fly
>   In the sky,
> Come and help me!

And then everything happened as before. The fairy dove and all the birds in the sky flew down, and in less than an hour the ashes were picked clean and the two pans were heaped high with peas.

Cinderella took them to her step-mother and said, "Now may I go?"

The step-mother flew into a rage and cried, "Don't be a fool! You have no dress to wear, and you could never dance in those clumsy clodhoppers of yours. You would disgrace us all."

With this she turned her back on the poor little girl and rustled off to the party with her two haughty daughters.

.   .   .   .   .

Cinderella did not mope and cry as you might suppose. Instead, she suddenly became very busy. She brushed the ashes out of her hair and combed it until it floated around

her face like a golden cloud. Then she scrubbed and
scoured herself until she was radiantly clean. No one would
ever have guessed that she was only a poor little kitchen
drudge who had to sleep among the ashes and cinders!
Now she ran out and stood under her hazel tree. As she
looked up into the leafy branches she said:

> Shake yourself, my little tree,
> Shower shiny clothes on me.

There was a whish and a whirr in the branches above,
and in that moment Cinderella's rags disappeared and a

shimmery silken dress fell over her instead. Her wooden shoes were gone, too, and on her feet were two tiny golden slippers. In her fluffy hair nestled a diamond star which sparkled in all the colors of the rainbow. Now Cinderella felt festive and gay, and she hurried off in high spirits to the party. When she appeared at the palace, she looked so rich and radiant that no one knew her, not even the step-mother and her haughty daughters.

As for the Prince, he had eyes for no one else from that moment on. He took her by the hand and did not leave her side all evening. Whenever anyone else wished to dance with her he always said, "No, she is my little dancer."

Cinderella was very happy, but she knew this happiness could not last long. The dove had warned her that all her lovely clothes would disappear at the stroke of midnight—and so, at a quarter of twelve, Cinderella was suddenly nowhere to be seen. When the Prince saw that she had disappeared, he looked frantically all over the palace, but he could find no trace of her anywhere.

In the meantime his little dancer had reached her own backyard. As she passed her hazel tree the clock struck twelve. Her shimmery clothes vanished, her tattered rags fell down upon her; and there she was, clumping into the house in her old wooden shoes. Once more she was only Cinderella, the poor little kitchen drudge!

Shivering in her rags, she lay down among the ashes and cinders as usual, but she was too excited to sleep. When the step-mother and her haughty daughters returned, Cinderella was still wide awake, and could hear them talking among themselves in the next room.

"That mysterious little beauty," said the step-mother, "who can she be, and why did she vanish so suddenly?"

"No one knows," said the first step-sister. "But I, for one, was glad she went. No one else has a chance with *her* around."

"Yes, I agree with you," said the second step-sister. "All the same I do wonder where she came from."

Little did they know that the maid of mystery had come from their home, and was at that very moment lying in rags and tatters among the cinders of their own hearth-stone!

. . . . .

The next day everything happened as it had before. The step-mother and her haughty daughters bedecked themselves in frills and furbelows and went, rustling and tinkling, to the ball.

Again Cinderella's tree showered shimmery clothes on her, only this time they were even more beautiful than before. As soon as she appeared at the palace, all eyes were upon her. The two step-sisters made wry faces, but the Prince rushed joyfully to Cinderella's side and would not leave her all evening. Whenever any one else wished to dance with her, he said, "No, she is my little dancer."

He was wildly happy, but to his dismay she gave him the slip again just before midnight. This time he saw her just as she was making her escape through the door. He ran after her, but she knew the way to her home, and he didn't. He often lost sight of her as she flitted in and out among the dark streets, but he kept on. He caught a glimpse of her as she turned into her own back yard, but it was so dark that he could not tell where she went after that. She had ducked in among the bushes and had reached her hazel tree at the stroke of twelve. Her beautiful clothes vanished, and when the Prince reached the tree, all he saw was a tattered little figure clumping into the house in wooden shoes. How could he guess that this was his dainty little dancer?

"But she ran into this yard, I saw her!" he said to himself. "She must be hiding here in the garden."

He searched every corner of the yard, parted every bush, and peered into every flower-bed, but of course his little dancer was not there. At last he went home, shaking his head sadly.

"But tomorrow it will be different," he said. "I'll see to it that she *can't* get away."

. . . . .

On the third evening, after the step-mother and her two haughty daughters had again gone off, rustling and tinkling, to the party, Cinderella stood under her magic tree as usual, and said:

> Shake yourself, my little tree,
> Shower shiny clothes on me.

She had no sooner said this, when a dress fluttered

down on her: a dress so heavenly fair that it must have been spun out of angels' dreams. A tiny crown, sparkling like a thousand dew drops, floated down and nestled in her hair; and two little golden slippers, set with dancing diamonds, fitted themselves neatly around her feet. But all these beauties were as nothing compared to her own winsome face, her modest air, and her graceful bird-like ways.

When she entered the palace, a hush fell over the hall; and the Prince, completely bewitched, dropped on one knee before her and kissed her hand. He would not leave her side all evening, and he smiled at her so happily and danced with her so gayly that Cinderella, blissful beyond words, almost forgot about the time. It was just *one* minute of twelve when she deftly drew her fingers out of the Prince's hand, ducked in among the many guests, and dashed away down the wide staircase which led to the street.

But the Prince, determined not to lose her again, had ordered the staircase to be painted with pitch, and as Cinderella skipped swiftly down the steps, one of her golden slippers sank into the pitch and stuck there! There was no time to spare, and Cinderella had to run off without the slipper.

At that moment, too, the clock struck twelve, her beautiful clothes vanished in a twinkling, and there she was, running down the stairs in rags and tatters. She had only just made her way through the big door when the Prince came tearing along, distracted and breathless. The guard, who had been half dozing, was rubbing his eyes.

"Have you seen my sweet little Princess?" cried the Prince.

"Princess?" said the guard. "Oh no, Your Highness."

"Has no one passed by here—no one?"

"Only a little beggar girl, Your Highness," answered the guard. "She was running for her life, but why, I don't know."

The Prince looked crestfallen and was about to turn back, when he spied the little golden slipper, caught in the strip of sticky pitch on the stairway. He picked it up, marveling at its dainty trimness. His eyes brightened.

" 'Tis true she got away from me," he said, "but I shall search until I find her, and this dear little slipper shall show me the way!"

Early the next morning he went to Cinderella's home and said to the step-mother, "I saw my little dancer disappear into your garden the other night—does she live here?"

The step-mother beamed with pleasure and her haughty daughters smirked and blushed with new hope.

"Here is something she lost last night," continued the Prince, as he drew the dainty little slipper from his pocket, "and only she who belongs to it can be my bride."

The oldest sister tried it on first. Her foot was narrow but too long. She had to nip off a bit of her big toe to get it in, but she didn't care—it would be worth it to be a Princess for the rest of her life!

When the Prince saw her wearing the slipper, he thought she must be the right girl, so he lifted her on his horse and started off with her to his palace. But as they passed the hazel tree, Cinderella's fairy dove called out:

Dee rookety goo
Just look at that shoe!

The Prince glanced down at the oldest sister's foot, and now he saw a little blood trickling out of the golden slipper. When he asked her to walk on it she could only hobble.

.   .   .   .   .

The Prince saw that he had made a mistake. He took her back and gave the second step-sister a chance. Her heel was too fat, so she had to nip off a little bit of it, but she didn't care. What was a little pain now, compared to the glory of being a Princess forever after? She squeezed her foot into the slipper, and the Prince lifted her on his horse, and started off. But as they passed the hazel tree, Cinderella's fairy dove called out:

Dee rookety goo
Just look at that shoe!

As the Prince glanced down he saw that the second sister's foot was fairly bulging out of the tiny golden slipper and that a few drops of blood were trickling out at the heel. When he asked her to walk on it, she could only hobble.

.   .   .   .   .

So he took her back home and said to the step-mother, "Is there another daughter in the house?"

"No, Your Highness," said the step-mother.

"No other girl?" said the Prince. "There must be! I saw one go into this house two nights ago."

"No, no," said the step-mother, "nobody but a clumsy

little kitchen maid. It wouldn't be she—I'm sure of that."

"Let me see her," said the Prince.

"Oh no, she's far too wretched and ragged to be seen by a Prince."

"Bring her out! It is my command!" said the Prince, and he looked at her so sternly that she had to obey.

Cinderella, in the kitchen, had heard all this, and had lost no time. She had washed and scoured herself and brushed the ashes out of her hair. As she entered, she lowered her head modestly, dropped a little curtsy and sat down on the chair which the Prince held out for her. She pulled off her clumsy wooden shoe, held out her trim little foot and slipped it easily into the tiny golden slipper which the Prince was holding in his hand.

Now she raised her head shyly, and when the Prince saw her fair face and looked into her kind starry eyes, he cried, "How could I ever have been mistaken! This is my own, my true little Princess indeed!"

At that moment, there was a whish and a whirr. No one knew how it happened, but Cinderella's rags had vanished and she was arrayed once more in her shimmery party attire.

The step-mother and her two haughty daughters were speechless with astonishment and fury. The Prince left them, snarling and sputtering among themselves, and walked out hand in hand with Cinderella. He lifted her beside him on his horse, and the young pair rode away happily through the garden. As they passed the hazel tree, the dove cooed:

> Rookety rookety goo,
> She is the bride for you!

It fluttered down and nestled on Cinderella's shoulder, and so all three—the Prince, his Princess, and her fairy dove—rode away, far far away, to a charming castle on a hill where they had a long and happy life together.

CLEVER ELSIE

CLEVER ELSIE

THERE was a man, he had a daughter who always tried to use her brains as much as possible and so she was called Clever Elsie.

When she grew up, her father said, "It is time to get her married."

And his wife said, "Yes, if only some one would come along who might want her."

At last from far away came one by name of Hans, who said, "Yes, I'll marry the girl, but only if she's really as clever as you say."

"Oh," said the father, "our Elsie is no fool."

And the mother said, "Ei, that's true. She is so clever, she can see the wind coming up the street. Yes, and she can hear the flies cough too."

"Well, we'll see," said Hans, "but if she's not bright I don't want her."

After they had all sat down at the table and had eaten something, the mother said, "Elsie, go down into the cellar and get us some beer."

At this the clever girl took the jug from the wall and trotted down the cellar stairs, clattering the lid smartly on the way, so as to be doing something with her time. Down in the cellar she brought out a little stool, put it in front of the cask, and sat on it, so she wouldn't have to bend over and perhaps unexpectedly hurt her back. Then she set the jug in front of the cask and turned on the tap. But while she was waiting for the jug to be filled, she did not want her eyes to remain idle, so she began busily looking around at the walls and ceiling. After much gazing hither and thither, what should she see right above her but a pickax which had been forgotten and left there by the masons! At this, Clever Elsie burst into tears, thinking: "If I should marry Hans and we should get a little baby, and he grows up and we send him down here to draw some beer, that pickax might suddenly fall down on his head and kill him."

So there she sat and cried with all her might over this possible accident.

Those up in the kitchen waited and waited for her, but she did not, did not come. At last the mother said to the hired girl, "Do go down into the cellar and see what's keeping our Clever Elsie."

When the girl went down and found Elsie sitting there, weeping so bitterly, she said, "Why are you crying like that?"

"Ach!" said Elsie. "Why shouldn't I cry? If I marry Hans and we get a baby and he's grown up and comes down here to draw some beer, maybe that pickax will fall on his head and kill him."

At this the hired girl said, "How can you think of all those things? Oh, what a clever Elsie you are, to be sure." So she sat down beside Elsie and began to cry, too, over the great misfortune.

.   .   .   .   .

After a time, as the hired girl did not return and those up in the kitchen were becoming restless and thirsty, the father said to the hired man, "You! Do you go down into the cellar and see what is keeping Elsie and the hired girl."

The hired man went down. There sat the two girls, both crying as though their hearts would break.

"What are you crying about, then?" asked the hired man.

"Ach!" said Elsie. "Why shouldn't we cry? When I marry Hans and we get a child and he's grown up and has to come down here and draw beer, this pickax might easily fall down on his head and kill him."

"Oh, what a calamity!" cried the hired man. "And what a clever Elsie you are, to be sure." So he sat down too, and kept them company with loud and anguished howls.

.   .   .   .   .

Above in the kitchen, the others were waiting for the hired man. As he didn't come and didn't come, the father said to the mother, "Wife, do you go down into the cellar and see where our Clever Elsie is staying."

The mother went down and found all three in the midst of loud lamentations. When she asked them the reason for such grief, Elsie explained that her future child would surely be killed, in case he should come down to draw beer just as the pickax might fall down on his head.

"Oh!" said the mother. "Who but our Clever Elsie could think so far ahead?" And she sat down and joined the rest in their sobs and howls.

. . . . .

The father up in the kitchen waited a while for his wife, but as she did not return either, he said, "Well, I guess I'll have to go down there myself and see what is keeping our Clever Elsie so long."

As he went down the cellar stairs and saw all four sitting there and crying, he asked them what was the matter. And when he heard that the reason for their grief was a child which Elsie might have some day, and which might be killed in case the pickax should fall down just at the time the child might be sitting there drawing beer, he cried, "Ah! That is foresight indeed! What a

127

Clever Elsie we have, to be sure." And he sat down and cried too.

·   ·   ·   ·   ·

Hans, in the meantime, stayed up in the kitchen for a long time but as no one returned, he said to himself: "They'll be waiting for you down there, no doubt. You'd better go down and see what they're about."

As he went down into the cellar there sat five, moaning and howling pitifully, one always louder than the next.

"What terrible misfortune has happened down here?" cried Hans.

"Ach, dear Hans!" wept Elsie. "If you and I get married and have a baby and he grows up and we might perhaps send him down here to draw some beer, that pickax might fall on his head and kill him. Isn't that something to cry about?"

"Well!" cried Hans. "That shows deep thought. More wisdom than this is not needful for my household and,

128

since you are really such a clever Elsie, I will marry you!"

He grabbed her by the hand, took her upstairs, and soon they were celebrating their wedding.

. . . . .

After Hans and Elsie were married and had a house and farm of their own, Hans said; "Wife, I must go out and earn some money. Do you go off into the field and reap the rye so that we may have bread."

"Yes, yes, dear Hans, that I will do," said Clever Elsie.

After he had gone she cooked up a good big broth and took it with her to the field. Once there, she sat down and began to use her brain as usual, for she wanted to be sure not to do the wrong thing. So she asked herself, "What shall I do? Shall I eat before I reap? Or shall I sleep before I reap? Hei! I'll eat first."

She sat down and ate up all the broth, and this made her almost too drowsy to move.

"I must put my clever brain to work," she thought to herself. "Now then, shall I sleep first or shall I reap first? Shall I reap or shall I sleep?" And so as not to waste any time while she was thinking, she began to cut down the grain.

She was now so sleepy she hardly knew what she was doing. While she was still saying, "Shall I reap? Shall

I sleep? Reap or sleep? Sleep? Reap?" she began to cut off her clothes, thinking it was the rye. Apron, shirt, skirt and kirtle: all were slashed in half. But Elsie did not know it—she was still asking herself the big question, "Shall I reap first or sleep first?"

At last she found the answer. "Hei, I'll sleep first!" she said, tumbled down among the rye-stalks, and was soon sleeping soundly.

When she awoke it was almost dark. She got up, and seeing herself all tattered and torn, and half naked besides, she did not know herself.

"I wonder," she said, "am I, I? Or am I not I?"

Try as she would, she couldn't find the answer, so she went on, "Now you! You're very clever and you ought to know. Think hard! Are you Elsie or somebody else?"

Still she didn't know.

At last the clever girl had an idea. "I know!" she said. "I'll go home and see if I'm there or not."

So she ran home and knocked at the window and said, "Is Clever Elsie there?"

"Yes, yes," said Hans, who thought she had come home long ago, "no doubt she's in her bed fast asleep."

"Ach!" cried Clever Elsie. "Then I'm already at home, and this is not I, and I'm not Elsie but somebody else, and I don't live here."

So she ran away, and no one ever saw her after that. But as she was such a clever girl and always knew what to do, I'm sure she got along very well wherever she went.

RAPUNZEL

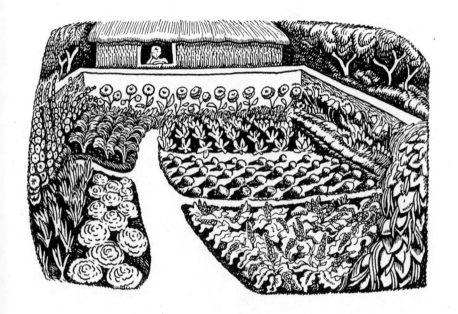

RAPUNZEL

IN a little German village lived a man and his wife. They had long wished for a child, and now at last they had reason to hope that their wish would be granted.

In their back yard was a shed which looked out upon their neighbor's garden. Often the woman would stand and look at this garden, for it was well kept and flourishing, and had lovely flowers and luscious vegetables laid out in the most tempting manner. The garden was surrounded by a high stone wall but, wall or no wall, there was not much danger of any one entering it. This was because it belonged to Mother Gothel, who was a powerful witch and was feared in all the land.

One summer's day, as the witch's garden was at its very best, the woman was again gazing from the window of her little shed. She feasted her eyes on the gay array of flowers, and she looked longingly at the many kinds of vegetables which were growing there. Her mouth watered as her eyes traveled from the long, crisp beans to the fat, green peas; from the cucumbers to the crinkly lettuce; from the carrots to the waving turnip tops. But when her glance fell upon a fine big bed of rampion (which in that country is called *rapunzel*) a strange feeling came over her. She had always been fond of rampion salad, and these plants in the witch's garden looked so fresh, so green, so tempting, that she felt she must have some, no matter what the cost.

But then she thought to herself, "It's no use. No one can ever get any of the witch's vegetables. I might as well forget about it."

Still, try as she would, she could not, could not for-

136

get. Every day she looked at the fresh green rampion, and every day her longing for it increased. She grew thinner and thinner, and began to look pale and miserable.

Her husband soon noticed this, and said, "Dear wife, what is the matter with you?"

"Oh," said she, "I have a strange desire for some of that rampion in Mother Gothel's garden, and unless I get some, I fear I shall die."

At this the husband became alarmed and as he loved her dearly, he said to himself, "Before you let your wife die, you'll get her some of those plants, no matter what the risk or cost."

Therefore, that evening at twilight, he climbed over the high wall and into the witch's garden. Quickly he dug up a handful of rampion plants and brought them to his ailing wife. She was overjoyed, and immediately made a big juicy salad which she ate with great relish, one might almost say with greed.

In fact she enjoyed it so much that, far from being satisfied, her desire for the forbidden vegetable had now increased threefold. And although she looked rosier and

137

stronger after she had eaten the rampion salad, in a few days she became pale and frail once more.

There was nothing for the man to do but go over to the witch's garden again; and so he went, at twilight as before. He had reached the rampion patch and was about to reach out for the plants, when he stopped short, horrified. Before him stood the witch, old Mother Gothel herself!

"Oh, Mother Gothel," said the man, "please be merciful with me. I am not really a thief and have only done this to save a life. My wife saw your rampion from that window yonder, and now her longing for it is so strange and strong that I fear she will die if she cannot get some of it to eat."

At this the witch softened a little and said, "If it is as you say, I will let you take as many of the plants as are needed to make her healthy again. But only on one condition: when your first child is born, you must give it to me. I won't hurt it and will care for it like a mother."

The man had been so frightened that he hardly knew what he was doing, and so in his terror, he made this dreadful promise.

RAPUNZEL

. . . . .

Soon after this, the wife became the mother of a beautiful baby girl, and in a short time Mother Gothel came and claimed the child according to the man's promise. Neither the woman's tears nor the man's entreaties could make the witch change her mind. She lifted the baby out of its cradle and took it away with her. She called the girl Rapunzel after those very plants in her garden which had been the cause of so much trouble.

Rapunzel was a winsome child, with long luxuriant tresses, fine as spun gold. When she was twelve years old, the witch took her off to the woods and shut her up in a high tower. It had neither door nor staircase but at its very top was one tiny window. Whenever Mother Gothel came to visit the girl, she stood under this window and called:

> Rapunzel, Rapunzel,
> Let down your hair.

As soon as Rapunzel heard this, she took her long braids,

wound them once or twice around a hook outside the window, and let them fall twenty ells downward toward the ground. This made a ladder for the witch to climb, and in that way she reached the window at the top of the tower.

Thus it went for several years, and Rapunzel was lonely indeed, hidden away in the high tower.

. . . . .

One day a young Prince was riding through the forest when he heard faint music in the distance. That was Rapunzel, who was trying to lighten her solitude with the sound of her own sweet voice.

The Prince followed the sound, but all he found was a tall, forbidding tower. He was eager to get a glimpse of the mysterious singer but he looked in vain for door or stairway. He saw the little window at the top but could think of no way to get there. At last he rode away, but Rapunzel's sweet singing had touched his heart so deeply that he came back evening after evening and listened to it.

Once, as he was standing there as usual, well hidden by a tree—he saw a hideous hag come hobbling along. It was old Mother Gothel. She stopped at the foot of the tower and called:

> Rapunzel, Rapunzel,
> Let down your hair.

Now a pair of golden-yellow braids tumbled down from the window. The old hag clung to them and climbed up, up, up, and into the tower window.

"Well!" thought the Prince. "If that is the ladder to the songbird's nest then I, too, must try my luck some day."

The next day at dusk, he went back to the tower, stood beneath it and called:

> Rapunzel, Rapunzel,
> Let down your hair.

The marvelous tresses were lowered at once. The Prince climbed the silky golden ladder, and stepped through the tiny window up above.

Rapunzel had never seen a man, and at first she was alarmed at seeing this handsome youth enter her window. But the Prince looked at her with friendly eyes and said softly, "Don't be afraid. When I heard your sweet voice, my heart was touched so deeply that I could not rest until I had seen you."

At that Rapunzel lost her fear and they talked happily together for a while. Then the Prince said, "Will you take me for your husband, and come away with me?"

At first Rapunzel hesitated. But the youth was so pleasant to behold and seemed so good and gentle besides, that she thought to herself: "I am sure he will be much kinder to me than Mother Gothel."

So she laid her little hand in his and said, "Yes, I will gladly go with you, but I don't know how I can get away from here. If you come every day, and bring each time a skein of silk, I will weave it into a long, strong ladder. When it is finished I will climb down on it, and then you can take me away on your horse. But come only in the evening," she added, "for the old witch always comes in the daytime."

Every day the Prince came and brought some silk.

The ladder was getting longer and stronger, and was almost finished. The old witch guessed nothing, but one day Rapunzel forgot herself and said, "How is it, Mother Gothel, that it takes you so long to climb up here, while the Prince can do it in just a minute—oh!"

"What?" cried the witch.

"Oh nothing, nothing," said the poor girl in great confusion.

"You wicked, wicked child!" cried the witch angrily. "What do I hear you say? I thought I had kept you safely hidden from all the world, and now you have deceived me!"

In her fury, she grabbed Rapunzel's golden hair, twirled it once or twice around her left hand, snatched a pair of scissors with her right, and ritsch, rotsch, the beautiful braids lay on the floor. And she was so heartless after this, that she dragged Rapunzel to a waste and desolate place, where the poor girl had to get along as best she could, living in sorrow and want.

.   .   .   .   .

On the evening of the very day in which Rapunzel had been banished, the old witch fastened Rapunzel's severed braids to the window hook, and then she sat in the tower and waited. When the Prince appeared with some silk, as was his wont, he called:

> Rapunzel, Rapunzel,
> Let down your hair.

Swiftly Mother Gothel lowered the braids. The Prince climbed up as usual, but to his dismay he found, not his dear little Rapunzel, but the cruel witch who glared at him with angry, venomous looks.

"Aha!" she cried mockingly. "You have come to get your dear little wife. Well, the pretty bird is no longer in her nest, and she'll sing no more. The cat has taken her away, and in the end that same cat will scratch out your eyes. Rapunzel is lost to you; you will never see her again!"

The Prince was beside himself with grief, and in his despair he leaped out of the tower window. He escaped with his life, but the thorny thicket into which he fell, blinded him.

Now he wandered, sad and sightless, from place to place, ate only roots and berries, and could do nothing but weep and grieve for the loss of his dear wife.

So he wandered for a whole year in deepest misery until at last he chanced upon the desolate place whither Rapunzel had been banished. There she lived in wretchedness and woe with her baby twins—a boy and a girl—who had been born to her in the meantime.

As he drew near, he heard a sweet and sorrowful song. The voice was familiar to him and he hurried toward it.

When Rapunzel saw him, she flew into his arms and wept with joy. Two of her tears fell on the Prince's eyes—in a moment they were healed and he could see as well as before.

Now they were happy indeed! The Prince took his songbird and the little twins too, and together they rode away to his kingdom. There they all lived happily for many a long year.

145

THE FISHERMAN AND
HIS WIFE

THE FISHERMAN AND HIS WIFE

THERE was once a fisherman and his wife. They lived together in a vinegar jug close by the sea, and the fisherman went there every day and fished: and he fished and he fished.

So he sat there one day at his fishing and always looked into the clear water: and he sat and he sat.

Then down went the hook, deep down, and when he pulled it up, there he had a big golden fish. And the fish said to him, "Listen, fisher, I beg of you, let me live. I am not a real fish; I am an enchanted Prince. How would it help you if you killed me? I wouldn't taste good to you anyway—put me back into the water and let me swim."

"Nu," said the man, "you needn't make so many words about it. A fish that can talk—I would surely have let him swim anyway."

With that he put him back into the clear water, and the fish went down and left a long streak of blood after him. And the fisher got up and went home to his wife in the vinegar jug.

"Husband," said the wife, "haven't you caught anything today?"

"Nay," said the man. "I caught a golden fish who said he was an enchanted Prince, so I let him swim again."

"But didn't you wish yourself something?" asked the wife.

"Nay," said the man. "What could I have wished?"

"Ach!" said the wife. "Here we live in a vinegar jug that smells so sour and is so dark: you could have wished us a little hut. Go there now and tell him—tell him we want a little hut. He will do that, surely."

"Ach!" said the man. "Why should I go there?"

"Ei!" said the wife. "After all, you caught him and let

him swim again, didn't you? He will do that surely; go right there."

The man still didn't want to go, but he did not want to go against his wife's wishes either, and so he went off to the sea. As he came there, the sea was all green and yellow and not at all so clear any more. So he went and stood and said:

> Manye, Manye, Timpie Tee,
> Fishye, Fishye in the sea,
> Ilsebill my wilful wife
> Does not want my way of life.

Now the fish came swimming along and said, "Nu, what does she want then?"

"Ach!" said the man. "After all, I caught you and let you go. Now my wife says I should really have wished myself something. She doesn't want to live in the vinegar jug any more; she would dearly like to have a hut."

"Go there," said the fish. "She has that now."

So the man went home and his wife wasn't sitting in the vinegar jug any more, but there stood a little hut and she was sitting in front of it on a bench. She took his hand and said to him, "Just come in. See, now isn't that much better?"

151

So they went in, and in the hut was a little hall and a
parlor; also a sleeping room in which stood their bed.
And a kitchen and dining room, with the best of utensils
laid out in the nicest way: pewter and brassware and all
that belonged there. In back of the hut was a little yard
with chickens and ducks, and a garden with vegetables and
fruit.

"See," said the wife, "isn't that neat?"

"Yes," said the man, "and so let it be. Now we will live
right contentedly."

"Nu, we'll think about that," said the wife.

With that they ate something and went to bed.

$\cdot \qquad \cdot \qquad \cdot \qquad \cdot \qquad \cdot$

So that went on for about eight or fourteen days, when
the wife said: "Listen, man, the hut is much too small, and

the yard and garden are so tiny. The fish might really have given us a bigger house. I want to live in a stone mansion. Go to the fish, he must give us a mansion."

"Ach, wife," said the man. "The hut is good enough— why should we want to live in a mansion?"

"Go there," said the wife. "The fish can easily do that much."

"Nay, wife," said the man, "the fish has already given us the hut. I don't want to go there again; it might displease the fish."

"Go!" said the wife. "He can do that right well and will do it gladly; you just go there."

The man's heart became heavy and he didn't want to go. He said to himself, "That is not right," but he went there anyway.

When he came to the sea, the water was all purple and gray and thick, and not green and yellow any more, but it was still quiet. So he went and stood and said:

> Manye, Manye, Timpie Tee,
> Fishye, Fishye in the sea,
> Ilsebill my wilful wife
> Does not want my way of life.

"Nu, what does she want then?" asked the fish.

"Ach!" said the man. "She wants to live in a big stone mansion."

"Go there then," said the fish, "she is standing in front of the door."

So the man left and thought he would go home, but when he reached it, there was a big stone mansion, and his wife was standing on the steps, just ready to go in. She took him by the hand and said, "Just come inside."

That he did, and in the mansion was a big hall with marble floors, and there were so many many servants, and they tore open the big doors. The walls were all bright, and covered with fine tapestries, and the rooms were full of golden chairs and tables. Crystal chandeliers hung from the ceilings, all the parlors and chambers were covered with carpets, and food and the best of wines stood on the tables so that they were ready to break.

In back of the mansion was a big courtyard with horse and cow stables, and carriages of the very best. Also there was a marvelous big garden with the most beautiful flowers and fine fruit trees. And a park—at least a half a mile long—in it were stags and deer and rabbits and all that one could ever wish for oneself.

"See?" said the wife, "isn't that beautiful?"

"Oh yes," said the man, "and so let it be. Now we will live in the beautiful mansion and be well satisfied."

"Nu, we'll think that over and sleep on it," said the wife. With that they went to bed.

.   .   .   .   .

The next morning the wife woke up first. It was just daybreak, and she saw from her bed the wonderful land lying before her. The man was still sleeping, so she nudged him in his side with her elbow and said, "Man, get up and just look out of the window. See? Couldn't one become

King over all that land? Go to the fish—we want to be King."

"Ach, wife!" said the man. "Why should we want to be King? I don't want to be King."

"Nu," said the wife, "if *you* don't want to be King, *I* want to be King. Go to the fish and tell him I want to be King."

"Ach, wife!" said the man, "that I don't want to tell the fish."

"Why not?" said the wife. "Go right straight there. I must be King!"

So the man went there and was right dismayed. "That is not right and is not right," he thought. He did not want to go but he went anyway. And as he came to the shore, there it was all blackish grey and the water foamed up from the bottom and it smelled all rotten. So he went and stood and said:

> Manye, Manye, Timpie Tee,
> Fishye, Fishye in the sea,
> Ilsebill my wilful wife
> Does not want my way of life.

"Nu, what does she want then?" asked the fish.

"Ach!" said the man. "She wants to be King."

"Go there then—she is all that," said the fish.

So the man went, and when he came to the mansion it had become a big castle. It had a high tower with wonderful trimmings on it, and a sentry stood before the door, and there were so many many soldiers with drums and trumpets! And as he came into the castle, he found that everything was made of marble and gold, with velvet covers and big golden tassels. Then the doors of the hall opened. There was all the court, and his wife sat on a high throne of gold and diamonds. She had a crown of pure gold on her head, and a scepter of gold and jewels in her hand. On both sides of her stood six maidens in a row, each always one head smaller than the other.

So he went and stood there and said, "Oh wife, are you now King?"

"Yes," said the wife. "Now I am King."

So he stood there and looked at her, and when he had looked at her like that for a while, he said, "Ach wife, how nice it is that you are King! Now we have nothing more to wish for."

"Nay, man," said the wife and looked all restless. "There

isn't enough to do. To me the time seems so long—I can't
stand that any more. Go there to the fish. King I am, now
I must also become Emperor."

"Ach wife!" said the man. "Why should you want to be Emperor?"

"Man," said she, "go to the fish. I want to be Emperor!"

"Ach wife!" said the man. "I don't want to tell that to the fish. He can't make an Emperor—that he cannot and cannot do."

"What!" said the wife. "I am King and you are my man. Will you go there right away? If he can make a King, he can make an Emperor. I want and want to be Emperor. Go there right now!"

So he had to go, but he became all scared. And as he went along like that, he thought to himself, "That doesn't and doesn't go right. Emperor is too much to ask for— the fish will get tired in the end."

With that he came to the sea. It was all black and thick, and began to ferment so that it made bubbles, and such a wild wind blew over it that the man was horrified. So he went and stood and said:

> Manye, Manye, Timpie Tee,
> Fishye, Fishye in the sea,
> Ilsebill my wilful wife
> Does not want my way of life.

"Nu, what does she want then?" asked the fish.

"Ach fish!" said the man, "she wants to be Emperor."

"Go there then," said the fish. "She is all that."

So the man went, and when he came there, the whole castle was made of polished marble with alabaster statues and golden decorations. In front of the door soldiers were marching, and they blew their trumpets and beat their drums and kettle drums. In the castle, barons and earls and dukes were walking around as servants: they opened the doors for him which were of pure gold. And when he came inside, there sat his wife on a throne which was made all of one piece of gold and was about two miles high. She wore a big golden crown which was three ells high and was set with brilliants and carbuncles. In one hand she held the scepter and in the other hand she had the imperial globe. On both sides of the throne stood the gentlemen-at-arms in two rows, one always smaller than the next: from the biggest giant who was two miles high, to the smallest dwarf who was only as big as my little finger. And in front of her stood so many many Princes and Kings!

So the man went and stood and said, "Wife, are you now Emperor?"

"Yes," said she, "I am Emperor."

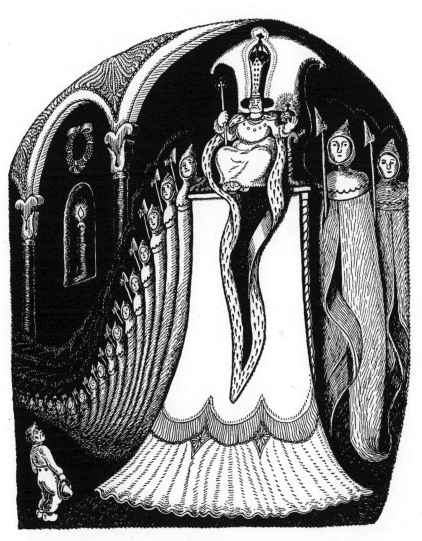

SO THE MAN STOOD AND SAID, "WIFE, ARE YOU NOW EMPEROR?"

So he stood there and looked at her right well, and after he had looked at her like that for a while, he said, "Ach wife, how nice it is now that you are Emperor."

"Man!" she said. "Why are you standing there like that? I am Emperor but now I want to become Pope. Go to the fish."

"Ach wife!" said the man. "What do you ask of me? You can't become Pope. There is only one Pope in Christendom; surely the fish can't make that."

"Man," said she, "I want to be Pope. Go right there. Even today I must become Pope."

"Nay, wife," said the man, "that I don't want to tell him; that won't go right, that is too much—the fish can't make you a Pope."

"Man, what chatter!" said the wife. "If he can make an Emperor, he can make a Pope as well. Get along. I am Emperor and you are my man—will you go there now?"

At that he was frightened and went there; but he felt all faint, and shook and quaked, and his knees and calves became flabby. And now such a big wind blew over the land, and the clouds flew so that it grew as dark as though it were evening. The leaves blew from the trees, the water

162

splashed against the shore, and worked and churned as though it were boiling. And far away he saw the ships; they were in trouble, and tossed and leaped on the billows. The sky was still a little blue in the middle, but at the sides it was coming up right red as in a heavy storm.

So he went there in despair, and stood in terror and said:

> Manye, Manye, Timpie Tee,
> Fishye, Fishye in the sea,
> Ilsebill my wilful wife
> Does not want my way of life.

"Nu, what does she want then?" asked the fish.
"Ach," said the man, "she wants to be Pope."
"Go there then," said the fish. "She is that now."

·　　·　　·　　·　　·

So he went, and when he came home it was like a big church with palaces all around it. There he pushed his way through the crowd: inside everything was lit up with

thousands and thousands of candles. His wife was dressed
in pure gold and sat on an even higher throne than before
and now she wore three big golden crowns, and all around
her there was so much pomp and grandeur! On both sides
of her, there stood two rows of candles: from the tallest, as
thick as a tower, down to the smallest kitchen candle. And

all the Emperors and Kings were down before her on their knees.

"Wife," said the man, and looked at her right well, "are you now Pope?"

"Yes," said she, "I am Pope."

So he went and stood and looked at her, and it was just as though he looked at the sun. After he had looked at her for a while, he said, "Ach wife, how nice it is now that you are Pope."

But she sat there stiff as a tree and did not stir or move herself. Then he said, "Well, wife, now that you are Pope you will have to be satisfied. You can't become anything more."

"That I will think over," said the wife.

With that they went to bed, but the wife was not satisfied, and her greediness did not let her sleep. She was always wondering what else she could become.

The man slept right well and soundly—he had done much running that day—but the wife could not sleep and tossed herself from one side to the other all through the night and wondered what else she could become, but could think of nothing higher.

With that the sun began to rise, and as she saw the
rosy dawn she leaned over one end of the bed and looked
out of the window. And when she saw the sun coming
up: "Ha!" she thought, "couldn't I, too, make the sun and
moon go up?"

"Man," she said, and poked him in the ribs with her
elbow, "wake up, and go there to the fish. I want to be
like God."

The man was still half asleep but he was so alarmed by this, that he fell out of bed. He thought he had not heard a-right and rubbed his eyes and said, "Ach wife, what are you saying?"

"Man," said she, "if I can't make the sun and moon rise and have to sit here and see that the sun and moon are going up, I can't stand that, and I won't have a peaceful moment until I can make them go up myself."

Then she looked at him in such a horrible way that a shudder ran over him.

"Go right there," she said, "I want to be like God."

"Ach wife!" said the man, and fell before her on his knees. "That the fish can't do. Emperor and Pope he can make. I beg of you, be satisfied and stay Pope."

At that she became furious and her hair flew wildly about her head. She lifted up her tunic and gave him a kick with her foot and screamed, "I can't stand it and I can't stand it any longer! Will you go?"

So he pulled on his trousers and ran away as though he were mad. But outside there was a storm and it raged so that he could hardly stay on his feet. The houses and the trees blew over and the mountains quaked. The big rocks broke off and rolled into the sea, and the sky was pitch black, and it thundered and lightened, and the sea went up into big black waves as high as church towers and mountains, and they all had a white crown of foam on their tops. So he screamed out and could hardly hear his own voice:

> Manye, Manye, Timpie Tee!
> Fishye, Fishye in the sea!
> Ilsebill my wilful wife
> Does not want my way of life.

"Nu, what does she want then?" asked the fish.

"Ach!" said the man. "She wants to make the sun and moon rise. She wants to be like God."

"Go home then," said the fish, "she's back in her vinegar jug again."

And there they are both sitting to this day.

THE THREE BROTHERS

THE THREE BROTHERS

A MAN had three sons and he was fond of them all. He had no money, but the house in which he lived was a good one.

"To which of my three boys shall I leave my house?" thought the old man. "They have all been good sons to me and I want to be fair to them in every way."

Maybe you think the simplest thing would have been to sell the house and then divide the money among the three boys. It would have been simpler but nobody wanted to do this. The house had been in their family for many years— not only the three boys, but their father, their grandfather, and their great-grandfather had been born in it. It was their home; they knew and loved every room, every window, every nook and cranny of it, and they could not bear to sell it to a stranger. So the old man had to think of a way out, and he did.

He called his three boys and said: "This is the way we'll do it. All of you must go out into the world. Each can choose a trade after his own heart and learn it well. In a year we will meet here together, and he who has learned his trade best shall have the house. Would you like to decide it that way?"

"Yes," said his sons, "that is fair enough."

And the oldest said, "I think I will become a blacksmith. That is the kind of work I like best."

"And I," said the second, "have always wanted to be a barber. That's what I'll set out to be."

"And I," said the third, "would like best of all to become a fencing master."

They agreed to return at the appointed time, and then they all went their separate ways. It happened, too, that they all found able masters who could teach them the higher branches of their trade.

The oldest boy became such a good blacksmith that he was soon hired to shoe the King's own horses. "Well," said the boy to himself, "I don't see how I can fail to win. I'll surely get the house."

The barber learned his trade so well that he was soon shaving all kinds of grand people: lords and earls and dukes. "Yes, yes," he said to himself, "this is not a bad beginning. The house is as good as mine right now, I think."

The youngest son endured many a blow while he was learning to fence, but he never winced or whimpered about it. "If you're so easily discouraged," he told himself, "you'll never get the house."

At last the year was up and they all returned to their father's house, but although each had become clever in his art, none could think of a good way to prove it. They were all sitting on a bench in front of the house to talk this over, when a rabbit came running over the field.

"Ei," said the barber, "that's as good as though I had called him."

He took his mug and soap, and quickly whipped up some suds while the rabbit was running toward them. Then, just as the rabbit ran past them at top speed, he lathered the little animal's chin and shaved it, leaving

enough fur for a stylish pointed beard. All this time the
rabbit had been running as fast as he could, and yet he
wasn't cut or hurt in any way.

"That pleases me," said the father. "Unless the others
do much better, the house will surely go to you."

Just then there was a buzzing in the air. The blacksmith looked up and said, "Ah, a gnat! That's just the
thing for me." And so, while the gnat was on the wing, the
smith quickly fitted it with little golden horseshoes, one
for each foot and each shoe fastened with twenty-seven
tiny nails. All this time the gnat had been flying around,
and everything was finished in a flash.

"You're a real fellow," said the father. "You've done

your work as well as your brother. At this rate I won't
know which of you ought to get the house."

In the meantime some dark clouds had been gathering
in the heavens and now a few drops of rain began to fall.
The youngest boy sprang up and said, "Well, I couldn't
have wished for anything better! Now I'll show you what
I have learned."

He stood up before them and, drawing out his sword,
he swung it in criss-cross strokes above his head and was
so deft about it that not a drop of rain fell on his head.
The rain came down harder, but the boy still swirled the
sword so swiftly that not a drop of rain could get by.
Yet harder fell the rain, faster and faster, until it seemed
as though it were being poured by tubfuls from the sky—
still his sword circled, swished and swirled. All around
him everything was wet, but he himself was as dry as
though he were standing under a roof.

When the father saw this he was astonished and said, "You have accomplished the greatest feat of all. The house is yours."

And the two older brothers—do you think they fought and quarreled about it? No, they were satisfied with the decision, for they, too, thought the youngest brother had been the best of all. But the young fencer did not want the house all to himself. He shared it with the others, and there they all lived happily together for the rest of their lives.

THE FROG PRINCE

THE FROG PRINCE

IN the olden days when wishing was still of some use, there lived a King. He had several beautiful daughters, but the youngest was so fair that even the sun, who sees so many wonders, could not help marveling every time he looked into her face.

Near the King's palace lay a large dark forest and there, under an old linden tree, was a well. When the day was very warm, the little Princess would go off into this forest and sit at the rim of the cool well. There she would play with her golden ball, tossing it up and catching it deftly in her little hands. This was her favorite game and she never tired of it.

Now it happened one day that, as the Princess tossed her golden ball into the air, it did not fall into her uplifted hands as usual. Instead, it fell to the ground, rolled to the rim of the well and into the water. Plunk, splash! The golden ball was gone.

The well was deep and the Princess knew it. She felt sure she would never see her beautiful ball again, so she cried and cried and could not stop.

"What is the matter, little Princess?" said a voice behind her. "You are crying so that even a hard stone would have pity on you."

The little girl looked around and there she saw a frog. He was in the well and was stretching his fat ugly head out of the water.

"Oh, it's you—you old water-splasher!" said the girl. "I'm crying over my golden ball. It has fallen into the well."

"Oh, as to that," said the frog, "I can bring your ball back to you. But what will you give me if I do?"

"Whatever you wish, dear old frog," said the Princess. "I'll give you my dresses, my beads and all my jewelry— even the golden crown on my head."

The frog answered: "Your dresses, your beads and all your jewelry, even the golden crown on your head—I don't

180

want them. But if you can find it in your heart to like me and take me for your playfellow, if you will let me sit beside you at the table, eat from your little golden plate and drink from your little golden cup, and if you are willing to let me sleep in your own little bed besides: if you promise me all this, little Princess, then I will gladly go down to the bottom of the well and bring back your golden ball."

"Oh yes," said the Princess, "I'll promise anything you say if you'll only bring back my golden ball to me." But to herself she thought: "What is the silly frog chattering about? He can only live in the water and croak with the other frogs; he could never be a playmate to a human being."

As soon as the frog had heard her promise, he disappeared into the well. Down, down, down, he sank; but he soon came up again, holding the golden ball in his mouth. He dropped it on the grass at the feet of the Princess who was wild with joy when she saw her favorite plaything once more. She picked up the ball and skipped away with it, thinking no more about the little creature who had returned it to her.

"Wait! Wait!" cried the frog. "Take me with you, I can't run as fast as you."

But what good did it to him to scream his "quark! quark!" after her as loud as he could? She wouldn't listen to him but hurried home where she soon forgot the poor frog, who now had to go back into his well again.

The next evening, the Princess was eating her dinner at the royal table when—plitch plotch, plitch plotch— something came climbing up the stairs. When it reached the door, it knocked at the door and cried:

> Youngest daughter of the King,
> Open the door for me!

The Princess rose from the table and ran to see who was calling her,—when she opened the door, there sat the frog, wet and green and cold! Quickly she slammed the door and sat down at the table again, her heart beating loud and fast. The King could see well enough that she was frightened and worried, and he said, "My child, what are you afraid of? Is there a giant out there who wants to carry you away?"

"Oh no," said the Princess, "It's not a giant, but a horrid old frog!"

"And what does he want of you?" asked the King.

"Oh, dear father, as I was playing under the linden tree by the well, my golden ball fell into the water. And because I cried so hard, the frog brought it back to me; and because he insisted so much, I promised him that he could be my playmate. But I never, never thought that he would ever leave his well. Now he is out there and wants to come in and eat from my plate and drink from my cup and sleep in my little bed. But I couldn't bear that, papa, he's so wet and ugly and his eyes bulge out!"

While she was talking, the frog knocked at the door once more and said:

Youngest daughter of the King,
Open the door for me.
Mind your words at the old well spring;
Open the door for me!

At that the King said, "If we make promises, daughter, we must keep them; so you had better go and open the door."

The Princess still did not want to do it but she had to obey. When she opened the door, the frog hopped in and followed her until she reached her chair. Then he sat there and said, "Lift me up beside you."

She hesitated—the frog was so cold and clammy—but her father looked at her sternly and said, "You must keep your promise."

After the frog was on her chair, he wanted to be put on the table. When he was there, he said, "Now shove your plate a little closer, so we can eat together like real playmates."

The Princess shuddered, but she had to do it. The frog enjoyed the meal and ate heartily, but the poor girl could not swallow a single bite. At last the frog said, "Now I've eaten enough and I feel tired. Carry me to your room so I can go to sleep."

The Princess began to cry. It had been hard enough to touch the cold fat frog, and worse still to have him eat out of her plate, but to have him beside her in her little bed was more than she could bear.

"I want to go to bed," repeated the frog. "Take me there and tuck me in."

The Princess shuddered again and looked at her father, but he only said, "He helped you in your trouble. Is it fair to scorn him now?"

There was nothing for her to do but to pick up the creature—she did it with two fingers—and to carry him up into her room, where she dropped him in a corner on the floor, hoping he would be satisfied. But after she had gone to bed, she heard something she didn't like. Ploppety plop! Ploppety plop! It was the frog hopping across the floor, and when he reached her bed he said, "I'm tired and the floor is too hard. I have as much right as you to sleep in a good soft bed. Lift me up or I will tell your father."

185

At this the Princess was bitterly angry but she picked him up and put him at the foot-end of her bed. There he stayed all night but when the dark was greying into daylight, the frog jumped down from the bed, out of the door and away, she knew not where.

The next night it was the same. The frog came back, knocked at the door and said:

> Youngest daughter of the King,
> Open the door for me.
> Mind your words at the old well spring;
> Open the door for me!

There was nothing for her to do but let him in. Again he ate out of her golden plate, sipped out of her golden cup, and again he slept at the foot-end of her bed. In the morning he went away as before.

The third night he came again. This time he was not content to sleep at her feet.

"I want to sleep under your pillow," he said. "I think I'd like it better there."

The girl thought she would never be able to sleep with a horrid, damp, goggle-eyed frog under her pillow. She

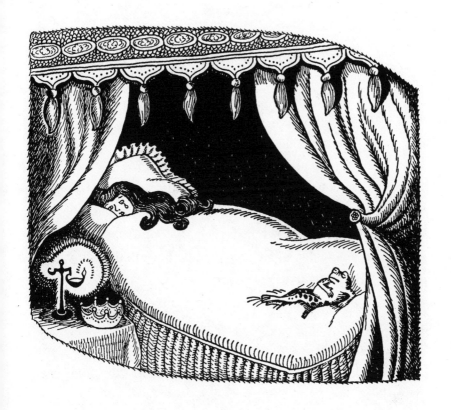

began to weep softly to herself and couldn't stop until at last she cried herself to sleep.

When the night was over and the morning sunlight burst in at the window, the frog crept out from under her pillow and hopped off the bed. But as soon as his feet touched the floor something happened to him. In

that moment he was no longer a cold, fat, goggle-eyed frog, but a young Prince with handsome friendly eyes!

"You see," he said, "I wasn't what I seemed to be! A wicked old woman bewitched me. No one but you could break the spell, little Princess, and I waited and waited at the well for you to help me."

The Princess was speechless with surprise but her eyes sparkled.

"And will you let me be your playmate now?" said the Prince, laughing. "Mind your words at the old well spring!"

At this the Princess laughed too, and they both ran out to play with the golden ball.

For years they were the best of friends and the happiest of playmates, and it is not hard to guess, I'm sure, that when they were grown up they were married and lived happily ever after.

LAZY HEINZ

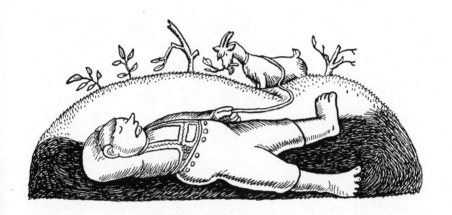

LAZY HEINZ

Heinz was a lazy fellow. He had nothing in all the world to do but drive his goat to pasture every day, and yet when he came home at night, he sighed and groaned.

"It is really a heavy task," he said, "and a toilsome business, yes! to take one's goat to pasture every day, year in, year out, from early spring, through the hot summer, way into the late autumn. And if one could only lie down and sleep while doing it! But no, one must keep his eyes open all the time, to see that the creature won't chew up young trees or get into someone's garden, or perhaps run away altogether! With all that to do, how can a fellow possibly get any rest, or enjoy his life to the full?"

He sat down, gathered his thoughts together, and considered how he might best free his young shoulders from such a burden. For a long time all his thinking was in vain, but suddenly a thought flashed into his noddle.

"I know what I'll do!" he cried. "I'll marry Fat Katrina across the way. She has a goat of her own. When she takes her animal out to graze she may as well take mine, and then I won't have to torture myself with all these hardships any more."

With that our lazy Heinz dragged himself to his feet. It took some time to bring his weary joints into action but at last he felt ready to walk. He ambled across the street to Fat Katrina's home and asked her parents if he might marry their good industrious daughter. Katrina's parents did not take much time to think this over. "Birds of a feather flock together," said they, and gave their consent.

So Fat Katrina became Lazy Heinz's wife. Every day she went away to herd his goat and hers, but Heinz lay late abed to rest himself from his long, long sleep of the night before. When he got up he did nothing but sit around and was well content to have it so. Only now and then he would go out on the hillside with Katrina and help her a bit with the herding.

"I'm only doing this work," he would say to her, "because my sleep will taste better after it—one must stop resting now and then, lest one lose all taste for it."

But Fat Katrina was just as lazy as her husband Heinz, and it was not long before she, too, became weary of herding the goats.

"Dear Heinz," said she one day, "why should we sour our lives with labor, use up our youth and tire ourselves out, when it isn't even necessary? Those goats disturb our best sleep every morning with their bleating—wouldn't it be better, Heinz, if we gave them to our neighbor and took one of his bee-hives in exchange? The bee-hive we could put in a sunny place behind the house, and pay no more attention to it after that. Bees don't have to be driven out and herded every day. They fly out alone, find their way home again all by themselves, and gather honey the whole day long without a bit of help from anybody. What do you think?"

Heinz sat up in bed.

"You've spoken like a sensible woman!" he said. "We will carry out your plan this very day. And do you know, Katrina, honey is very nourishing. Besides, it tastes better than goat's milk, and keeps better too—it never gets sour."

Their neighbor was willing enough to trade a bee-hive for two goats, and Lazy Heinz and Fat Katrina were more than pleased over the bargain.

The bees did their work well, flew in and out, back and forth, from dawn till dark every sunny day. They filled the hive with fine sweet honey, and in the autumn there was more than the bees could use themselves, so Heinz was able to take out a whole jar-full of honey for himself and Katrina.

They put the honey jar on a shelf over the bed. But, as they were afraid it might be stolen by either mice or men, Katrina cut a stout hazel stick and kept it beside her bed. In this way she could chase away unwelcome guests without even getting up to do it.

Life was now very sweet for the lazy pair, and Heinz could never see any use in getting up before noon. "He who rises too early," he would say, "frets all his blessings away."

One day as he was thus busy preserving his blessings, lying snug among the feathers at noontime, he said to Fat Katrina (who was still in bed too, giving herself a much needed rest after her long night's sleep)—"Wife," he said, "women have a weakness for sweets, that we know. And I know that you are nibbling at that honey off and on. Before you eat it all up yourself, wouldn't it be better to trade it in for a goose and some goslings?"

"Well, yes," said Katrina, "but not before we have a child to herd them. Why should I worry myself with a flock of geese and use up my strength unnecessarily? Let the child do the work."

"Ho! Do you think our child will herd geese?" cried Heinz. "Nowadays children don't mind their parents any more. They think they are wiser than their elders and do just as they please."

"Oh no!" said Fat Katrina. "It will go hard with our child if he doesn't do as we say. A good stout stick—that's what I'll take, and I'll let him feel it too, if he doesn't mind us. See, Heinz?" she cried, picking up the hazel stick in her excitement. "See? This is the way I'll spank him!"

She raised the stick above her head, but unluckily in

195

doing so, she hit the honey jar which stood above the bed. The jar fell down and broke, and the good sweet honey flowed over the floor.

"Well," said Heinz, as he leaned over the side of the

bed and looked at it, "there lies our flock of geese now— and that's the end of that task; they won't have to be herded after all. But Katrina! Isn't it lucky that the jar didn't fall on my head? We can well be thankful that things turned out as they did."

His head was still hanging over the side of the bed as he spoke, and now he noticed a little pool of honey in one of the broken fragments. He reached out after it and said in deep contentment: "What's left of the honey, wife, we'll eat and enjoy. And then we'll lie back and rest ourselves so that we may recover from this frightful experience. What difference will it make if we get up a little later than usual? The day will still be long enough."

"Yes," said Fat Katrina, as her head sank back among the downy pillows, "there's always plenty of time to get anywhere, and haste will get us nowhere."

"Yes, it is better to take it easy," said Heinz, so they both went back to sleep once more.

LEAN LIESL AND
LANKY LENZ

LEAN LIESL AND LANKY LENZ

VERY different from Lazy Heinz and Fat Katrina—
who never allowed anything to disturb their rest—was
Lean Liesl. Instead of taking life easy, she toiled and
moiled from morn till night, and found so much work for
her husband, Lanky Lenz, that he was more burdened
than a donkey with three sacks. But it never did them
any good, for in spite of all their toil and trouble, they
had nothing, and got nowhere.

One evening as she was lying in bed, so worn and weary

that she could hardly move, Liesl still could not sleep—her thoughts and worries kept her wide awake.

After much thinking she sat up in bed, nudged her husband in the ribs with her sharp elbow, and said, "Do you know, Lenz, what I've been thinking? Suppose I should find a florin and somebody should make me a present of another; then I would borrow a third, and you would give me a fourth. As soon as I had these four florins all together, I would go and buy a young cow."

This idea pleased the man, but he said: "I really don't know where I would get the florin you want me to give you; but if, for all that, you can gather so much money together and can get a cow for it—why then you will do well to carry out your plan."

He lay there and thought a while and then he continued, "I will be pleased, too, when the cow has a little calf, for then I will sometimes be able to refresh myself with a drink of milk."

"The milk isn't for you," said Lean Liesl. "That's all for the calf so it can grow big and plump, and so that we will get a good price for it."

"Oh yes, of course," said Lanky Lenz, "but we could

take a very little of the milk for ourselves; that would surely do no harm."

"Who ever taught you anything about raising cows?" cried Lean Liesl. "Whether it does any harm or not, I won't have it, that's all! And even if you stand on your head for it, you won't get a drop of milk. You long lanky Lenz, just because you're always hungry and can never get filled up, is that a reason why you should have the right to eat up all my earnings?"

"Wife!" cried Lanky Lenz. "Be quiet or I'll box your ears for you!"

"What!" cried Lean Liesl. "You want to threaten me, you glutton, you insatiable string-bean, you long lanky lout?"

She pounced on him and tried to tear his hair. But Lanky Lenz rose up, grabbed her skinny arms with one hand, and with the other he pushed her head back on the pillow. That's the way he held her, and like that he let her scold until, all tired out, she fell asleep at last.

Whether Lean Liesl went on scolding when she woke up the next morning, or whether she went out to look for the florin she wanted to find, that I don't know.

SNOW WHITE AND
ROSE RED

SNOW WHITE AND ROSE RED

A POOR widow lived in a little cottage, in front of which grew two rose trees. She took such good care of these little trees that they blossomed all summer long, one with white and the other with red roses.

She had two children, both girls; and, because they reminded her of the beautiful roses in her garden, she called one Rose Red and the other Snow White.

Rose Red, with dark hair and rosy cheeks, was full of life and fun; and she liked to romp in the fields and meadows. Snow White had flaxen hair, was quiet and gentle, and was happiest when helping her mother with the housework.

But although the two girls were so different in their ways, they were the best of companions and loved each other dearly. And when Snow White said, "We will never leave each other," Rose Red would answer, "No, never." Then their mother would add: "Whatever one has, must be shared with the other." And the sisters always did so.

Often they would go hand in hand into the woods to gather flowers or red berries. All the creatures of the wood knew them well and did them no harm. Little rabbits ate greens out of their hands without fear, wide-eyed deer grazed peacefully at their side, and the birds never flew away when they came, but stayed in the trees nearby and sang all they knew.

Sometimes the two children would wander in the woods, forgetting all about the time, until it was nightfall. Then they would lie down on a bed of soft moss and sleep soundly until morning. They were never afraid, and their mother did not worry about them, for she knew that the kind creatures of the forest would protect them.

At home in their little cottage, each girl had her own work. In the summer time Rose Red kept house. She always got up at sunrise and, before she did anything else, she would pick a white and a red rose and set them at her mother's bedside for a morning greeting. In the winter time Snow White took care of the house. She too would get up early, and then she would make a good warm fire in the hearth and hang a shiny kettle on to boil.

In the summer evenings, when the day's work was at an end, mother and daughters would sit in the doorway to look at the sunset and the flowers. But in the long winter evenings, when the big flakes fluttered softly and silently about the doors and eaves, the little family gathered snugly about the fireside: the mother reading tales of mystery and magic from the big old book on her knee, and the two girls spinning softly, listening in rapt wonder. At their feet lay a pet lamb, and behind them on a swinging bar sat a white dove, dozing in the warmth with its head tucked under a wing.

One evening as they all sat together like this in cozy contentment, there was a knock at the door. The mother said, "Quick, Rose Red, open the door. That must be a poor wanderer, looking for shelter from the snow and wind."

Rose Red drew the bolt and opened the door. At first she thought it was an old man out there, but it wasn't. It was a bear who pushed his big black head in at the kitchen door. Rose Red sprang back, the pet lamb bleated, the dove fluttered on its perch, and Snow White hid behind her mother's bed.

But the bear could talk and he said, "Don't be afraid; I won't hurt you. I am half-frozen and only want to come in for a little while until I am warm again."

"You poor bear!" said the mother. "Lie down by the fire, but be careful not to scorch that furry coat of yours."

Now Rose Red and Snow White came forward and looked at the huge creature; even the lamb and the dove lost their fear and settled down in their places as before. The bear looked around and said, "You children, come and beat the snow out of my fur."

Rose Red and Snow White brought their brooms and swept his shaggy pelt until it was clean and dry. As for the bear, he seemed to like it; and when he was well brushed off, he stretched himself beside the fire and grunted with satisfaction.

Although he looked so rough and sounded so gruff, he was a gentle bear, and so good-natured that the two girls were soon romping merrily with him. They tickled and teased him, tousled his fur and tumbled about with him as though he were a big dog. Sometimes as he lay on the floor, they planted their feet on his wide back and rolled him from side to side; at other times they spanked him playfully with a hazel whip. When he growled they laughed, for they knew he really didn't mind it—but sometimes when they forgot themselves and spanked him a little too much, he said:

> Spare my life, Snow White, Rose Red,
> He who is dead can never wed.

The children did not know what he meant, so they only laughed, but they stopped spanking him when he said it.

When bedtime came, the mother said to the bear, "You can stay right here on the hearth. There you will be good and warm all through the night."

The bear was glad enough to do this, but the next morning when Snow White arose to light the fire, he asked her to let him out. She opened the door and he trotted off through the snow into the depths of the forest.

From that time on the bear came every evening at the same hour, lay down by the hearth and let the children tumble and tussle with him as much as they liked. Soon

211

they became so used to him that they never even thought of bolting the door until their big black playfellow had arrived.

When springtime came and things were fair and green once more, the bear said to Snow White one morning, "Now I must leave you all, and won't be back all summer and fall."

"But why are you going, and where, dear bear?" asked Snow White.

"I must go to the woods," said the bear, "and guard my treasure from the thievish gnomes. In winter when the earth is frozen hard, they must stay in their homes in the ground, for they can't work their way out. But now that the warm sun is thawing up the earth, they will soon break through and come out to filch and steal. Anything which once gets into their caves or grottos will not easily find its way back into the light of day. And so, dear friend, I must go."

Snow White, feeling sad at this farewell, was half in tears when she pulled the bolt for him. As the bear pushed his shaggy bulk through the door, he was caught on the door-hook; and, as he did so, a piece of his hide was ripped away. It seemed to Snow White that a bit of gold shimmered through the rent; but, because of her tear-dimmed eyes, she couldn't be sure. The bear trotted away in a great hurry and was soon lost among the trees in the forest.

Some time after this, the mother sent Snow White and Rose Red into the forest to gather brush wood for the kitchen fire. There they saw, not far away, a big fallen tree on the ground. Something was bobbing up and down on its trunk but, because of the grass and weeds, they could not tell what it was. As they reached the place, they saw it was a gnome. He had a wrinkled greyish face, and a white beard at least a yard long. The tip of this beard was caught in a cleft of the tree-trunk, and the little man was jumping up and down like a dog on a chain, but couldn't get free. He glared at the girls with his red fiery eyes and cried, "Why are you standing there like fools? Can't you come and give me a helping hand?"

"But how did you get caught like that, little mannikin?" asked Rose Red.

"Stupid, snoopy goose!" cried the gnome. "This tree— I was going to cut it up into kindling for my kitchen fire. I can't use big chunks; they always burn up the tiny dinners and suppers which we little people eat. We're not like you; you big, greedy people who eat so much and gulp things down in hunks. Well, I got the wedge into the tree, and all was going well, but that confounded piece of wood was so slippery that it sprang out. Then the cleft in the tree closed so suddenly that my beautiful white beard got caught in it. There it is now! I can't pull it out and can't get away. And there you stand and laugh, you weak-minded, sleek, and silly, milk-faced fools. Phoo! I hate you!"

The children did the best they could for the little gnome, but they could not get his beard out of the cleft; it was caught too tightly.

"I'll run and get some people to help us," said Rose Red at last.

"Blockheads!" screamed the gnome. "Who wants any more silly mortals around here? There are two too many of you here as it is. Can't you think of something better?"

"Now don't be so impatient," said Snow White in her gentle way. "I've thought of something else."

She took her scissors out of her pocket and snipped off the tip of the gnome's beard. As soon as he was free, the little man grabbed a sack of gold which was lying among the roots of a tree nearby. As he lifted it out he grumbled to himself, "Vulgar folk! Here they cut off my magnificent beard. May the cuckoo get them in the end."

With that he flung the sack on his back and went off without another look at the two girls.

A few days later, the two sisters went out to catch some fish for their supper. As they neared the pond they saw something which looked like a big grasshopper jumping towards the water as though it meant to get into it. They hurried forward and saw it was the gnome.

"Where are you going?" asked Rose Red. "Surely you don't want to go into the water?"

"I'm not such an idiot!" screeched the gnome. "Can't you see that fiendish fish is trying to drag me into it?"

"Oh, that's too bad," said Snow White kindly. "But how did you ever get into such a fix, little mannikin?"

"What business is it of yours, you nosy impudent thing?" cried the gnome. "I was sitting there angling peacefully enough, when the wind tangled up my beautiful beard with that confounded fish-line. Just then I had a nibble; but the fish was too big, I couldn't pull him out. And now instead of letting me catch him, he's after me, and is trying to drag me into the water, the fiend!"

As he was scolding away, the little fellow was clinging to everything in his path, stones and weeds, twigs and reeds and rushes; but it did not help him much. The fish had the upper hand, and the gnome would surely have been drowned if the two girls hadn't come in the nick of time.

They threw down their fishing lines and ran to help him. Rose Red held on to him while Snow White tried to undo the snaggy mass of beard and fish-line. But it couldn't be done; it was too much of a tangle. There was nothing to do but get out the scissors once more. Very carefully Snow White snipped a bit here and there. When she had freed him, only a very little of the beard was gone, but the ungrateful fellow yelled out in fury, "Is that right? Is that mannerly? You clumsy spiteful things! Not enough for you that you lopped off the lower half of my marvelous beard, now you've also cut away most of what was left! I'm so disfigured I won't dare to show myself to my kith and kin. Such clouts, such country louts! Meddlers, that's what you are!"

He picked up a sack of pearls which lay among the rushes and, without another word, he dragged it off and disappeared into a hollow beneath a big stone.

Soon after this, the mother sent her two daughters off

217

to town to buy some things she needed: thread, ribbons, needles and twine. Their way took them over a rock-strewn meadow; and, as they were walking along, they saw a big bird soaring in the air above them. It was an eagle. He was circling slowly, and gradually coming lower and lower. At last he landed beside a big rock not far from them, and pounced on something. At the same time there rose an anguished piercing cry. The sisters ran over to the spot and were horrified when they saw that the little gnome, their old acquaintance, was hanging help-lessly in the talons of the big eagle.

In spite of his ungrateful scolding ways, the two girls felt sorry for the little fellow, so they caught hold of his clothes, and tugged and pulled and scuffled around so long with the eagle that at last the bird gave up the struggle and released his prey.

As soon as the gnome had recovered from his terror he shrieked out as usual in his shrill voice, "You lumps, you clumps! Couldn't you have handled me a little more care-fully? Look at my clothes! My elegant little coat, my fine trousers—you've ripped them into strips, rude awkward rabble that you are!"

He picked up a sack of jewels which was hidden behind a clump of weeds, and slipped away under a rock into his cave.

By this time Rose Red and Snow White were used to his churlish ways and, without thinking any more about it, they went on their way.

On their return they came upon the gnome once more. He had not expected any one to come by so late in the evening, and had emptied the sack of jewels on the ground. They were glowing and sparkling magnificently in the rays of the setting sun—the two girls were speechless with wonder and stood there gazing wide-eyed at the sight.

When the gnome saw them he shrieked, "You apes, you gaping boobies! Why are you standing there like that?" And his ash-grey face turned fiery red with fury. He was about to go on scolding, when a loud grumble was heard, and a big black blear trotted out of a thicket at the edge of the meadow.

Frightened, the gnome leaped up and tried to run away to his secret lair. But the bear was already upon him and the little gnome cried in anguished tones: "Bear, dear bear, oh spare me—and I'll gladly give you all my treasures.

219

See those gems lying there? And in my cave under the rocks are gold and pearls besides. Give me my life! What would you have with a lean little, lank little fellow like me? You couldn't even feel me between two of your teeth. There, take those two worthless girls—they'll be juicy morsels for you, plump as quails. Eat them instead of me!"

The bear paid no attention to these words. He merely gave the malicious fellow a tap with his huge paw so that he never stirred again.

The girls had sprung away but the bear called out to them, "Snow White, Rose Red! Don't be afraid. Wait, I want to go with you."

When they heard his voice the girls knew it was their dear old friend, the bear, so they waited. As soon as the bear had reached them, his shaggy black hide fell off and there stood a handsome youth clad all in gold.

"I am a King's son," he said, "and was bewitched by that wicked gnome. Not only did he turn me into a bear but he stole all my treasures besides. But that is all over now."

He took Snow White for his bride, and Rose Red married his brother. Together they shared all the treasures which the gnome had stolen and hidden in his hollow.

The mother lived for many years quietly and happily with her two children. But the two rose trees she took with her. They were planted just outside of her window and bore each year the most beautiful blossoms, white and red.

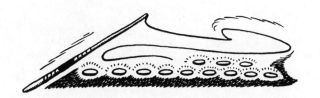

THE DRAGON AND HIS
GRANDMOTHER

THE DRAGON AND HIS
GRANDMOTHER

ONCE there was a war. The King who had waged this war had many soldiers; but although he was glad enough to let them fight and die for him, he was not willing to pay them enough to live on. At last three of his soldiers put their heads together and decided to run away.

"But how shall we manage it?" said one. "If we get caught, it's the gallows for us."

"Do you see that rye-field?" said another. "We'll sneak over there at dusk and hide in it for the night. Tomorrow the army will move on and then we can make our escape with safety."

But things did not go that way. Orders were changed and the army stayed on day after day. The three run-away soldiers in the rye-field waited and waited—without food, without water. They dared not come out of hiding and it looked as though they would have to die there of hunger and thirst.

At last, who came? A fiery dragon came flying along and lay down in the field, coiling himself in and out among the rye-stalks.

"Soldiers, eh? Why are you hiding here?" asked the dragon.

"We ran away from the King's army," said the soldiers, "because he paid us so very little money for so very much fighting. But here we are, dying of hunger. We can't go out after food, for we would surely be captured and that would be the end of us."

"Hm! Hm!" said the dragon. "I can save you, my good lads; and I'll do it gladly, too, if you'll promise to serve me for seven years."

The soldiers looked at each other doubtfully, for they did not like the idea of having a dragon for a master.

"Still," said they to one another, "we have no choice.

After all, anything is better than dangling on the gallows
or starving miserably in this rye-field."

So they promised.

The dragon seized them in his claws, flew through the
air high above the army, and carried them far from the
encampment. He set them carefully on the ground and
gave them each a little whip, saying: "Snap these whips,
gentlemen, and gold will spring out of the air like grass-
hoppers. The more you snap the whips, the more money
you will have. See, my friends? You can live like lords
and have no end of fun. This will be your life for
seven years. At the end of that time I will ask you
a riddle. If you guess it, you can keep your whips and
I will have no further power over you. But if you fail,
you will belong to me forever after."

The soldiers shuddered a little, and when the dragon
asked them to sign their names in his book, their hands

trembled. But as soon as the dragon had flown away they forgot their fears. Quickly they snapped their whips, and hui! the gold sprang out of the air and lay in shiny yellow heaps about them.

Now the three lads started off on a carefree journey. They went here, there, and wherever their fancy led them. What a merry time they had, snapping their whips, gathering in the gold, and living in style! They bought fine clothes, elegant carriages and prancing steeds. They were good-hearted fellows, never harmed any one, shared their gold with one and all, and spread gayety wherever they wandered.

Well, so it went for seven years, with a hi ya ya! and a hup sa sa! But as their time drew to a close, two of the soldier-lads became sad and fearful. The third soldier was not afraid. He was a light-hearted fellow and he said: "Come, come, my comrades. Don't worry about it. I didn't fall on my head when I was a baby—I've got my wits about me—and I'll find an answer to the dragon's riddle when the time comes."

But the other two were not very hopeful. They sat there with drooping mouths and long faces, looking as gloomy as a wet week, when who should come hobbling along but an old granny? She saw how sad they were and asked them what their trouble was.

"What can it matter to you, little old mother?" said the soldiers. "Surely you can't help us."

"Who knows?" said the granny, wagging her head. "Who knows? Come, tell me all about it and we'll see."

When she had heard their story, she said: "Now, now, my lads, that's not as bad as it might be. I can tell you what to do. One of you must wander in the woods until he finds a big cliff. In one side of it is a cavern which looks like a home. This he must enter and there he will find help."

The two doleful ones thought, "We'll never be saved that way," and went on moping. But the light-hearted one tossed his cap into the air, caught it again and cried, "Many thanks, little old mother. I'm off!"

He wandered all day, and toward nightfall he came upon something which looked like a cave-home in the side of a cliff. He peered in at the door and saw an old, old, *very* old woman. The soldier-lad wished her the good of the evening, and the old woman was so pleased with his

229

merry, honest face that she asked him to come in and sit down. They chatted for a while and, just think, the soldier found that he was talking to the dragon's own grandmother! She did not like her grandson very well, and she *did* like the merry soldier-lad; so when she heard his story she took pity on him.

"It's getting dark," she said, "and my dragon-boy will soon be home. Hide here," she added, lifting up a flat door in the floor over the cellar. "Be as quiet as a mouse and prick up your ears. You may hear something which will help you in your trouble."

The soldier-lad did as he was told, and soon the dragon came flying along. He crowded himself into the cave and demanded some dinner. The old woman spread out a mighty repast which put the dragon in great good humor.

"Well, my boy," said the grandmother, "and how have things been going with you?"

"Oh," said the dragon, "not much luck today. But why should I care? In a few days I *will* have some fun. Listen to this, grandma. Seven years ago I signed up three soldier-lads, and he he! hei hei! their time is almost up!"

"Are you so sure you'll get them?" asked the grandmother. "They might be too clever for you."

"Oh no!" shouted the dragon gleefully, with plenty of
smoke coming out of his nostrils. "Oh no, grandma. I've
got a good riddle for them—they'll never guess it."

"And what kind of a riddle may that be?" asked the
grandmother as she filled up his bowl again.

The dragon gave another smoky snort and said: "I'll
tell you. It's a good one. In the great North Sea lies

231

a dead long-tailed monkey—that's to be their roast meat. The rib of a whale shall be their spoon, and an old hollow horse-hoof shall be their wine glass. Isn't that good? He he! Ha ha! Ho ho!"

And he went to bed in high glee.

Now the old woman lifted up the cellar door and the soldier stepped softly out of his hiding place.

"Did you hear what he said?" whispered the grandmother.

"Yes, thank you, my good woman," said the lad. "I heard everything clearly."

He hurried back to his companions and told them what had happened. Now all three were wild with joy, and snapped their whips right and left, so that the money sprang about like hailstones in a storm.

A few days later the seven years were up and the

dragon appeared. He pointed to the three names in his book and said, "You promised!"

"Yes, we promised," said the soldiers, trying not to look cheerful.

'And so now for the riddle," continued the dragon. "I know you'll never guess it and you're as good as mine already."

"Well then?" said the soldiers.

"Well then," said the dragon, "I will take you to my dominions, where I will give you a feast. And what do you think you'll have for roast meat?"

Said the first soldier-lad: "In the great North Sea lies a dead long-tailed monkey. I suppose that's to be our roast meat."

The dragon was taken aback.

"Hm! Hm! Hm!" he muttered. "But what's to be your spoon?"

Said the second soldier-lad: "The rib of a whale—I dare say that's to be our spoon."

The dragon made a wry face.

"Hm! Hm! Hm!" he muttered again. "But can you guess what shall be your wine glass?"

Said the third soldier-lad: "An old hollow horse-hoof— that's to be our wine glass, like enough."

The dragon turned purple with fury.

"Hu! Hu! Hu!" he roared, and flew quickly away, for well he knew that he had lost all his power over them.

The three soldier-lads were now free forever. They were merry and carefree once more, snapped their whips for gold as before, and if they haven't stopped they're at it still.

IN CASE YOU WANT TO KNOW—

*The meanings or pronunciations of the unusual
words in this book*

Ach!—there is really no English word to rhyme with it,
but the Scotch word *loch* comes near to it. Say it with
a strong *h* ending (not *lock*), then leave off the *l* and
you'll be close to the right pronunciation of *ach*. It is
an exclamation meaning, *Oh! Ah!* or *Alas!*

Bremen—like *bray-men,* with the accent on the *bray.*

Ei, Ei!—it's pronounced just like *I, I!* and is an exclamation meaning *Well, well!* or *Well, indeed!*

Fishye—instead of saying *ye fish*—just turn it around and
say *fish-ye.* The accent is on the first part, and it means
little fish.

Gothel—like *goat-l.*

Gretel—like *Grate-l.*

Gretl—same as *Gretel.*

Hans—there is no English sound like the *a* in **Hans**. It doesn't rhyme with *fans*, nor with *tons*, nor with *dons*. If you say it like *hunts*, you're fairly close to it.

Hansel—the same problem as **Hans**. **Hunnsel** is the closest sound-spelling I can give you.

Hei!—like *High!* Used like *Hey!*

Heinz—say it to rhyme with *pints*.

Hu! Hu! Hu!—just like *Who! Who! Who!* This is an expression of horror.

Hulla!—the first syllable rhymes with *dull*. An expression of surprise or worry.

Ilsebill—like *Ill-ze-bill*, with the accent on the first syllable.

Katrina—pronounced **Ka-treen-a**, with the accent on *treen*.

Lenz—rhymes with *dents*.

Liesl—this rhymes with *measle*.

Manye—like two words, *man ye*, with the accent on the *man*. It means *little man* because the fish really was a man—an enchanted one.

Nottage—this is just a sound-word, and doesn't mean a thing —like "Hickory, dickery, dock" which doesn't mean anything either.

Nu, Nu!—like *Noo, noo*. It means *Well, well!* or *Well, now!*

IN CASE YOU WANT TO KNOW

Rapunzel—it should really be said as though it were written *Ra-poon-zel,* but if you prefer, you can pronounce the middle part like the word *pun.* In any case, the accent is on the middle syllable.

Timpie Tee—say it just the way it's written. In a way it doesn't mean a thing—that is, it's not a dictionary word —but it's a magic one, so you see it's very important, all the same.

Best known for her Newbery Honor winner *Millions of Cats*, WANDA GÁG (1893–1946) was a pioneer in children's book writing, integrating text and illustration. Born in New Ulm, Minnesota, she rose to international acclaim. In recognition of her artistry, she was posthumously awarded the 1958 Lewis Carroll Shelf Award for *Millions of Cats* and the 1977 Kerlan Award for her body of work. Her books *The ABC Bunny*, *The Funny Thing*, *Gone Is Gone*, *More Tales from Grimm*, *Nothing at All*, *Snippy and Snappy*, and *Snow White and the Seven Dwarfs* are all available from the University of Minnesota Press.